VIDUI

DAVID R. SLAVITT

LIVINGSTON PRESS
THE UNIVERSITY OF WEST ALABAMA

Hardcover binding by: HF Group
Typesetting and page layout: Sarah Coffey
Proofreading: Joe Taylor
Cover art: Susan Ludvigson
Cover Layout: Nick Noland

first edition

6 5 4 3 3 2 1

VIDUI

For Janet

A Jew's final prayer, it is recited when death is imminent. The Vidui (vi-DOO-ee) is not so much a confession, although that is the usual translation of the Hebrew word, as an acknowledgment. Having lived a life, you may be prompted to give thanks for it or repent of it. But either way, an acknowledgement of some kind is appropriate. Celebration and lamentation are unreliable, because they so much depend on the mood of the moment or one's habitual predisposition—one's mental weather or climate. Death is an occasion that demands a more realistic attention, serious and just. This is what I am attempting here—honesty.

Strangely, the quality of the prose does not much matter. Style is a vanity, and I am no longer trying to impress anyone or to be pleasing. Awkwardness, too, has a truth to convey. I admit that I tinker with the sentences now and then, but only as a way to achieve clarity and wrest from them whatever interesting implications may be lurking among their obstinate syllables.

I have spent my life doing this, constructing an *other*, a non-me with which I can struggle in the hope of achieving some understanding and even perhaps a degree of refinement. Nevertheless, with a solitary self, there can be no real dialogue or Talmudic *pilpul*, and I have to admit that decades of this activity of mine have produced little in the way of wisdom. At best, there were momentary insights I had, surprising and satisfying but not, alas, memorable. Or not memorable enough for me to remember.

But was there an alternative?

§

To acknowledge the world should not be so difficult a philosophical or aesthetic endeavor: give me a place to stand and I should be able to manage it, if not actually to move the earth. Or give me a place to stand and I'd rather not. I'd prefer to sit. Silly? Candor requires me to admit to silliness. Even to assert it vigorously. Wordplay is an intimate habit I have to try to control when I am not alone. When I am, silliness is a way of fending off stillness. It can also be a useful tool. "When Thou has done, Thou hast not done (Donne), / for I have more." More sins, he means: the line is the refrain of "A Hymn to God the Father," which is Donne's version of the *Vidui*. If the Dean of St. Paul's could combine such punning with the fervor of his prayers, I can surely cut myself a pair of slacks.

My eldest child is sixty now, but I remember him at three or so, saying "Supper, super, supper, super... superintendent." It was like watching him roll over for the first time or take his first unsteady steps. ("Superintendent" was not an exotic word for a child living in an apartment house in Manhattan.) Words are mostly useful, but for bright children they are also toys. And this wasn't just a cute mistake ("Praise Beater God!") but a discovery, authentic albeit minor.

I do not understand theoretical physics, but it seems to call attention to the observer's point of view. From what angle is this true, and when, and does the very act of observation involve a distortion? Schrödinger's cat is simultaneously alive and dead until you open the box and look inside, at which instant it is one or the other. This is a *Gedankenexperiment* of Erwin Schrödinger's and my interest in it is not in the logic of the paradox but only the cat, because Erwin would be such a great name for one. (Who would get it? But that would be the point, exactly: it would be a joke, apparently innocent, but then not so innocent, a put-down for less mentally agile or less well-informed people. It is unkind but I confess to having done such things from time to time.)

Schrödinger is in his box and definitely dead. He has been since 1961, but the cat, being a fiction, still lives and will forever. The principle that observation itself affects the result is relevant here because the prayer's meaning arises from the one who is praying. God is always the same, as are the words of the prayer, but each of us is different. Aren't we?

The assumption that there is a set formula by which the dying acknowledge their lives at the very least de-emphasizes their individuality, which they are in any event at the point of losing. We recite the prayer and by so doing belatedly join (or rejoin) family, congregation, tribe, and ultimately mankind. The details of the life matter less and less as we merge into the generality of humanity. We say: "We have transgressed, we have acted perfidiously, we have robbed, we have slandered. We have acted perversely and wickedly, we have willfully sinned, we have done violence, we have imputed falsely. We have given evil counsel, we have lied, we have scoffed, we have rebelled, we have provoked, we have been disobedient, we

have committed iniquity, we have wantonly transgressed, we have oppressed, we have been obstinate
…"

Some of us have done some of those things, and
others, others. But very few have committed all of
them. It makes no difference however as we leave the
corruption of the world for the further corruption
of the grave. (Metaphors are dangerous.) It is a serious moment, and yet I know myself well enough
to wonder whether some of my neurons may per-
sist even then in behaving badly. "The worms play
pinochle on your snout," is distressing as it flashes
across my consciousness. We have oppressed, we
have been obstinate, we have been embarrassing…
(Is that perversity enough?)

It must happen to others that such stray thoughts
intrude, irrelevant if not so defiantly frivolous. But I
have no choice and take what comes. The charm of
the line is in the word "pinochle" with its alliteration
of the p in "play." And "snout" is appealing, also, picturesque and rhyming with "the worms crawl out."
The image is somewhere between H. Bosch and W.
Disney. No one gathered around the bed has any idea
that I am off on such a tangent. This is both a relief
and a disappointment to me, because it means that
even members of my immediate family don't know
me well enough to intuit such a thing. Or they don't
know me at all.

There is a Yale Online Course on "Death," in
which Shelly Kagan, an elfin professor of philosophy,
argues that the saying "We die alone" is not necessarily true—and in some ways, his arguments are difficult
to refute. He points out that those who die in suicide
pacts, or in catastrophes like battles, plagues, famines,
tsunamis, plane crashes, and volcanic eruptions have

4

company in their demise. Where I think he gets it wrong is that we also live alone. (His argument here is that the aloneness is therefore not unique to death. And my response would be that it is only when we are facing death do we realize the depth of the isolation in which we have lived, sadly, all along. So we may not be more alone when we are about to die but we feel it more.) The saying only applies, then, to those who know that they are dying. (But who doesn't?) Strictly speaking, when we face death we do so alone.

But however we untangle that problem, there is a singular and irreducible inner self we never reveal to other people, a kernel of personhood that is the repository of all our secrets. Even the friendliest, most gregarious, and most beloved people have from time to time a sense of isolation. It is in that persistent and inescapable solitude that we live and die and it is that inner being for which we mourn as our minds and bodies try to maintain their diminishing functionality.

Clear the room, then, of weeping relatives who are mostly a distraction, put on a kippah and a tallit, wash your hands (three times!), and then recite the prayer: *"Modeh ani l'fonecha…"* "Modeh" means, roughly, acknowledge. And *"Ani"* is the first person singular pronoun, which is important because after *l'fonecha* (before you) the prayer immediately changes to the first person plural. ("We have transgressed, we have robbed, and we have acted wickedly…") This shift to the plural indicates that the prayer no longer comes solely from the dying individual but from and for the minyan, the congregation, the entirety of Israel. The whole broken world, even. These collectives are what we are fading into. No longer are they merely the furtive and subversive thoughts of which we are about to rid ourselves but all thoughts, as if death were a cold body of water into which we venture a cautious toe, hoping to adjust gradually. This would account for the mention of sins the dying person has not committed. Have I robbed? Have I done violence? No, but some of us have, and the focus of the confession has now been broadened.

Is that what it means? Jews are good at grammar so it is unlikely to be a mistake. And in any case, we can tease meaning out of almost anything. Or am I whistling up the wrong tree of knowledge? Or barking, I should say. It's frogs that whistle up in trees. There must have been frogs in paradise.

§

These secrets need not be large or important. Small privacies work in the same way. I used to wonder why in so many movies and lately even TV programs men confide in each other as they stand at adjacent urinals. How does urinating underscore the significance of the dialogue? The implication is that the two of them are being candid with each other. This has become as much a cliché as the overturned fruit carts in high-speed chases. I can't remember which film it was that had a scene in which an older man was taking a leak alone, not into a urinal but an ordinary toilet, and he didn't just stand there but leaned forward and braced himself against the wall to let gravity help him empty his bladder without dribbling on his pants. There was a ripple of laughter in the theater from men, each of whom had supposed that this trick was his alone and was slightly shocked by the small, recognizable truth and the realization that what each thought was his secret had now been revealed to the world so that women and younger men knew about it, too. For old men, peeing and also not peeing are important concerns, but few novelists have referred to these things, as they might do if only in the interest of verisimilitude.

Pissonyu, pissonyu, pissonyu. / *In Russian this means, "I love you."*/ *If I had my way, I'd pissonyu all day*...I don't remember the next line, but the shape of the stanza suggests that there must have been one. Schoolboy humor. I remember singing the song on a day trip a few of us made to the Cape in the early fifties, a couple of girls, two other guys, and me. We were all in prep school and were packed into a large red convertible I'm pretty sure had cream-colored leather upholstery. One of the other guys, Larry something, took it upon himself to write to my parents to complain about my crudeness. Extraordinary! I hate to imagine what his toilet training must have been like. That he became a psychiatrist is not surprising. O Lord, have mercy on his patients.

There. That is—or was—a secret, if only because it wasn't funny enough or important enough for me ever to tell anyone. The others in the car are all dead, and when I go, the incident will be gone, too, along with a host of other such moments, some embarrassing or shameful, some sad, and some splendid. They will have merged with the universal confession or acknowledgement of the prayer. Even transgressions I have entirely forgotten will be represented, and in that thought there is some small solace.

§

My relationship with prayer, this one or any other, is uneasy, which is perhaps a good thing. Just to recite the words and become a kind of whirling Indian prayer wheel or flapping Tibetan flag isn't what most of us aspire to. There ought to be a self, as authentic as possible, offering the prayer. With me, the self makes its presence known, first of all, by my limited fluency in Hebrew. I understand less than most of the congregants around me, and this reduces some of the phrases to nonsense. But I believe in the nonsense—those wisps and fragments of Hebrew that circulate in my head. They make up in sincerity what they lack in meaning. *Shantih, shantih, shantih*, Eliot wrote at the end of "The Waste Land," and I always have to fight to keep that from turning into "Shampoo, shampoo, shampoo," which I did once as a joke but which now presents itself as an attractive alternate reading. Nutty, but then not so nutty because both words are derived from the same Indian language. Hindi? Kashmiri? Konkani, Malayalam? Guajarati? Tamil? Pali? Sanskrit, even? (I do not remember anyone having a shampoo in *The Mahabarata*, and I think I'd have noticed it.) Such an abrupt descent to domesticity reminds me of Milton's effort in that direction when, in *Paradise Lost*, the angel comes to chat with Adam and Eve and, in an oddly considerate moment, Milton writes, "no fear lest dinner cool," which is memorable only for its weirdness. Did Eve cook? Had they somehow discovered fire? And were there frogs, which aren't kosher but which one can eat and even survive on? One would think that the French were accustomed to famines. Why else would they have been driven to include frogs' legs and snails in their culinary repertoire? Where were we? I was talking about my uneasy relationship to prayer. And nonsense. With a Rowley, powley, gammon and spinach, Heigh ho, says Anthony Rowley. V'imeru, amen.

Odd names some of those frogs have—Anthony

and Ebenezer. Kermit, of course. And Dan'l Webster, Mark Twain's celebrated jumping frog. Jeremy Fisher in some Beatrix Potter story. And I think one of J. K. Rowling's Harry Potter books has a frog named Trevor. "'O Mistress Mouse, are you within?'/ 'Can a frog fuck a mouse?' she replied with a grin." We have gone far afield, even allowing that she might have been a field mouse.

You have a phenomenal intelligence (otherwise you would not still be reading this), excellent taste, and a quick wit, too, I dare say. Also you are very patient, and I thank you for that. I expect that you have already come to a tentative diagnosis—that my problem is merely an attention deficit disorder. But don't say that or think it as if it were a bad thing. It isn't a lack of capacity with me but a low tolerance for pain and boredom that continued attention to almost anything in the outer world is likely to cause (outside my head, outside the room in which I lie on that deathbed we have been imagining, experiencing terminal ennui). I could pay attention, but as Bartleby, my fellow scrivener, keeps saying, "I would prefer not to."

I don't care about sports. If I want to know what the weather is, I look out of the window. Good or bad, financial news is frightening. And the lead stories are generally unspeakable. (From headlines you can get lead poisoning.) What useful comment can there be about a massacre of children? "It happens." That's hardly adequate, and tender souls may think it irreverent, but it is the best the talking heads can come up with, although they disguise it as information by comparing it with the latest half dozen mass shootings, as if the death tolls were in some way competitive. The news of the maniac's regrettable childhood and his dreadful deeds is unbearable enough without this further bit of dopey contextualization.

I have the feeling of not being from here. (Which is always a good answer if somebody asks you the time.) The natives speak a language I sometimes think I understand. They seem to behave themselves, but I might as well be from a distant planet. Lest they find me out (And tear me apart? And eat me?), I find it safer to retreat as far as I can to the interior where Mistah Kurtz is in critical condition. The brevity of my attention span is a well-developed defense mechanism, an evasive stratagem that has served me well. It avoids unpleasantness by keeping me from dwelling too long anywhere, with anyone, on anything.

Can you blame me?

Do I care?

§

Death itself is uninteresting. We know nothing about it and its nothingness is impossible to imagine. That "undiscovered country from whose bourn no traveler returns." Bourn in the sense of boundary, but it also can mean an intermittent stream. With an e tacked on, it is a town down on the Cape, named after Jonathan Bourne, who became rich in the whaling business.

Deathbed scenes are vividly in our minds because of the many nineteenth-century sentimental descriptions in prose and paint of the touching moment with the family gathered around the elderly, defunctative paterfamilias. They affect to be sad, he pretends to be comforted. Our own fears may be ever so slightly assuaged by the contemplation of what the writer or artist has set before us. My own preference (and I am in charge here) is to allow the geezer propped up on the pillows to be considering the life he has lived, however well or badly. He would not discuss this with the family and friends surrounding the bed. Indeed, he hasn't the faintest idea whether they are there out of sadness or respect or as the first gambit in what will be a sordid, drawn-out wrangle over his estate. He therefore cannot trust the expressions on their faces or the words they say—at this moment or, as he realizes, any previous ones, which makes it more difficult to consider his life and the part he has played in the lives of others. He cannot trust his own guesses either, because he knows by now that these are based on faulty data and are almost certainly a function of his passing mood. Or the mood of his passing. (He makes jokes, too, I see, but then he is my improvisation.)

Perhaps even he is feigning, as in *Volpone*. Any attempts at communication are treacherous. Thought itself is treacherous. In which case, the problems of communication recede toward the vanishing point. But never mind, for if we cannot do anything about these difficulties, what good does it to do worry?

His name, of course, is Vernon Dewey although he generally signs letters as V. Dewey. No? Too much? There was some great musician whose advice to a young conductor was to protract the final chord just a little longer than good taste would allow. Which do you want, then, truth or good taste? And yes, you have to choose. We have to choose. I have to choose. I am about to have chosen…(How often do we come across future perfects?) I have chosen. Truth. Or Consequences. There's a city in New Mexico actually called that, even though the radio program for which it was named is long gone and mostly forgotten. (I do remember that the host was Raoul Phèdre, or something like that.) The town's name is so cumbersome and embarrassing that the locals refer to it as "T. or C." One of the embarrassing curiosities of Les Etats Zuni, it is near Elephant Reservoir, which is so named because elephants used to come there to drink and spray each other in hot weather.

§

This last was Dewey's suggestion. Blame him. (Easy enough for me to say.) But we should indulge him at least a little, *in extremis*. And *in flagrante*. And *in loco parentis*, too. His mind, at the brink of the void, is vertiginous and tries to retreat. With all its strength and cunning. It is a futile undertaking, however, and there is the risk that, for no reason apparent to anyone else in the room, he will break into laughter. (Has he lost his mind? Can we use that to try to break the will? We should look that up in Schopenhauer's authoritative textbook on testamentary practice.) The case would become well known and would be cited, as Dewey v Dewey. (Again? He is playing orthopedist with us, pulling our leg!)

Schopenhauer said, "Truth is no harlot who throws her arms around the neck of him who does not desire her; on the contrary, she is so coy a beauty that even the man who sacrifices everything to her can still not be certain of her favors." This may not tell us much about truth but it suggests that Schopenhauer was a seriously disturbed fellow whose life and work give new meaning to the idea of a committed philosopher. I am horsing around. (Do horses make jokes? Do they play?) Arthur—as his friends called him, if he had friends—also wrote: " "Unless suffering is the direct and immediate object of life, our existence must entirely fail of its aim."

If there were a company that made anti-Hallmark cards, he could run it. Schope and Hauer, maybe?)

Striking as they are, these were not his last words. Having the last word can mean that you've won an argument. Or that you're dying. (Or that your adversary has died?) There are anthologies of last words, some of which are entertaining. Oscar Wilde spoke wittily of the wallpaper. Chekhov said that he hadn't drunk champagne in a long time. Max Jacob, peculiar to the end, asked if anyone had a toothpick. Gertrude Stein is supposed to have said, "What was the answer? What was the question?" Maybe, but it is not cynical to wonder whether Alice B. Toklas didn't make that up later and attribute it to her companion, not from mischievousness but as an embellishment, an enhancement. They had edited each other's work, hadn't they? And there was no reason to draw the line at words when, at least on this occasion, she could edit reality, too, a loftier and more strenuous endeavor. (You can think of it simply as lying, but that is less interesting.)

What has any of this to do with the solemn prayer? Everything! One is not only considering one's life but also still living it, and these irrelevant thoughts are a part of it. We may dismiss them as distractions from the dark pit at Vernon's feet. But what, at this moment, is any more relevant than anything else? Such an ordering is pretentious and arbitrary. Vernon has lost patience with it, as patients will. The prayer? Is in the book on the nightstand, but God has heard it before and has no need of another iteration. Its presence on the printed page should be sufficient—like the texts in mezzuzot, offering up their continual blessing for anyone who crosses the threshold. "And thou shalt bind them for a sign upon thy hand, and they shall be for frontlets between thine eyes. And thou shalt write them upon the doorposts of thy house, and upon thy gates." People kiss them as they pass through the doorway. On Sabbath mornings, before and after the readings from the Torah, a procession winds its way up and down the aisles of the synagogue with someone carrying the scrolls so that members of the congregation can reach out and touch one of them with their tallit fringes or the siddurs they have kissed. This isn't something a person usually does to inanimate objects, but the Torah is life, is animation itself. And if we do not believe this or cannot, we can at least, for the sake of appearances, pretend.

Another way to think about that curious procession through the shul is that the kisses are an exchange. If we kiss the Torah, it is reasonable to suppose that the Torah is reciprocally kissing us. Not a sexy kiss but the kiss-and-make-up kind. Or at least the ceremonial parental or the French hello. It is an inarticulate enactment of the confession of the *Vidui*.

§

So what kind of guy has Vernon been? As he lies there, he is as close to an abstraction as a character can be. Musil's *Man Without Qualities* has more qualities. Shall we describe him, give him a scar here, a mole there, a receding hairline (the hair used to be more or less auburn but is now silvery white)? It would be beside the point, which is that he no longer looks like himself. Or anyone living. The fat has drained from his cheeks and chin, and his head is now a skull with skin covering it loosely. Eyes, of course, but they are closed most of the time. Nose and mouth with the thin lips somewhat dry, despite the nurses' efforts to apply lip balm (with natural peppermint flavor). What is most interesting about him is that along with the change in his looks, there has been a gradual dissolution of his personality. Back in the day when he was witty and a bit caustic, he might have asked if the dissolution of his body was a metaphor for what was going on in his mind or was it the other way around? The old baboon by the light of the moon was combing his auburn hair, except that it wasn't auburn anymore. And in the next line is the monkey who gets drunk, the same creature as the baboon, who is in a different family?

He has a name, but only as a result of that dreadful pun on *Vidui*, which is, so far as I know, the only sin of which he so far has to repent. He has a template family gathered around him, none of whom are baboons. Some of them appear to be praying, others have their attention fixed on him in a posture intended to express dignified grief rather than mere curiosity. But even if we had more in the way of a detailed history or even a physical description, what difference would it make? The window is open, presumably to allow his departing soul an easy passage into the next world. Or is it just stuffy? Or malodorous? You may choose. I don't care. The advantage of my vagueness is that it invites the reader to project himself into this sad business and Vernon's ectoplasmic existence in the bed where the declivities in the pillow and mattress are nearly as substantial as he is.

An odd thing about dying is that nobody knows how to do it. We can't practice for it and thus are all beginners. We can't even carry out some plan for it that we may have formulated once in an idle moment of self-pity. We are obliged to improvise and some do so more gracefully than others. Or maybe they just have better luck. My hope is to die in my sleep, even though that means my wife will wake up to find herself lying beside a corpse. A hell of a way to start the morning, isn't it? Before she has had a chance to pee and brush her teeth!

But Vernon hasn't "passed" yet. That's the frequent euphemism for "died," and while it avoids the dread word, it carries its own batty implication—that it is a kind of exam for which we have been preparing for years and finally will have "passed?" (Often the passing grade is "the big C.") But the locution more frequently is "passed over," or "passed on." "Passover" means precisely the opposite, for if you have lamb's blood on your doorpost or upon your gates, the angel of death will pass over your house and take ("smite," even) only the Egyptians, all of whom will have to pay dearly for their dear Pharaoh's invincible obstinacy.

Anyway, he's not dead yet, our Vern. He hasn't even begun to produce that death râle that will frighten the family members around his bed who have never heard it, unless some of them happen to be hospice nurses. They get used to it—almost. (I cannot imagine one of them recording that sound to use on her phone as a ring tone, except that, as you see, I have just imagined it. And having done so, I checked and strike me dead if it isn't available on YouTube.)

§

Poor Vernon has no privacy left. He has been infantilized to the point where first he needed help to urinate into the vase (I'm using the nurses' word for it, but I'm enjoying it more than they do.) And he needs assistance to move his bowels into the bedpan and get cleaned up afterward. And then, as if that hadn't been bad enough, there was the diaper and its mess. That unendurable process prompts further moments of dissociation, an escape to an alternate universe that is less of an affront. No privacy, no dignity. No hope, no point. No bananas. And although it is impending, there seems to be no end to any of it. These are all humiliating assaults on his dignity and what he had taken to be his minimal self, the core of the core.

What is left then but his secrets, or not even the secrets so much as the burden of keeping them? But "burden" is not quite right. Weightiness, more like. An anchor, actually. It is said that secrets alienate us from the rest of the world, but alienation can be a good thing, an assertion of an individual self that has not yet been diapered and tranquilized into death's blurry generalizing welcome.

It need not be a secret of great moment. I think of the old countess in *Pique Dame*, with her secret formula of the three winning cards at faro. Herman tries to force her at gunpoint to tell him, but she dies of shock and takes the secret to her grave. (Dramatic ironing, as the women down in the *laverie* call it.) And then? Her ghost appears to tell Herman what the three cards are; only she lies, which is one way of keeping a secret. Dopey Herman goes off confidently to wager everything he has and, believing that now he can't lose, bets on those cards, the three, the seven, and the ace. But wouldn't you know? The third card he turns up is the queen of spades. (Not altogether a surprise, given the name of the opera.) He sees the ghost of the countess laughing at him and in a moment of pique says, "Damn!" Then he kills himself.

So he transports himself into the past tense because her wraith's wrath has persisted and her vengeance is triumphant. Ridiculous of course, but it's an opera, which means that however extravagant its machinery, there may be some underpinning of plausible human truth.

(Faro? That's what the libretto says, and I rely on that. Did the Israelites ever play faro in Egyptland? No? Okay.)

What secrets could Vernon have been keeping in the tangled neurons in his head? All kinds, big and small, happy and sad. You lose some, of course, as your memory lets go, but as you get older, there are more and more recollections of conversations and interactions that become your exclusive property. As the others die off, you become the sole keeper of these moments, because it is only in your life, your breath, and your flesh that they retain even a shadowy existence. No one else, not even close friends who are visitors in your house, can tell that the lamp on that highboy used to be in your mother's bedroom. That is, unless you choose to disclose it.

You may forget a lot but with the right cues from the randomness of the world, some things come back. Meanwhile, as friends, acquaintances, and also people you disliked pop off, the store of unique recollections you have inherited grows almost every day. One of the advantages of the role of exclusive proprietor is that no one can correct you or disagree with you. There is no one left who knows or cares, so if you modify a bit here or there to make the recollection a little more interesting, the edited version becomes the truth.

Lately, Vernon has not bothered to read the obituaries, the section of the paper to which (until recently) he turned first, because that was the only real news. He was like one of those noblemen who has a chart on the wall and with each death gets closer to inheriting the throne of the country that is at least as real as the one out the window. The monarch of all he surveys, even if monarchs generally hire professional surveyors to go out with their tripods and transit-levels to do the actual work. (But then he is the monarch of them, too.)

Who will even have any notion that Vernon thinks about such things and, indeed, has been doing so for decades? Even though we are imagining him without the obstacles the real world puts in the way of such intimate knowledge, what do we know of him? Do I know what my children think? Or my wife? My parents are dead, so I can invent for them without worrying about accuracy. Whatever I put into their notional heads is all there is, although it resonates sometimes in a sepulchral setting and sounds more authoritative than when they were alive—which I didn't value highly enough because it was merely real. Harsh words to and from living people fade. The dead have memories that preserve some conversations and moments forever, but then they have metamorphosed altogether into those memories like lumps of coal that have become diamonds.

When he was dying, my father could not speak. He had apparently had a stroke along with everything else. He could write, though, and his last note to us— my mother, my sister, and me—was on a scrap of paper in a shaky, spidery hand quite unlike his beautiful Palmer cursive. What he managed to scrawl was:

"terrible pain." I kept the piece of paper as a kind of relic but I have moved several times since then and the paper has been lost. (He has taken it back? No.) The words, however, are still with me although I have lost many of his previous pronouncements, exhortations, warnings, and reproaches over the decades, which is a kindness to both of us.

I must assume that Vernon is in the same position and that he has retained sounds and images he'd rather have lost. If you have a choice in life between good manners and honesty, take the former. Decorum is less chaotic and less stressful, which is why it evolved in the first place. If civilization cannot achieve at least some semblance of civility, it is nothing but barbarity in French cuffs.

The Dewey family is rather subdued, not because of the old man in the bed, but rather because in one another's presence they wish not to seem boorish. Individually, they may be having disgraceful thoughts and feelings, some frivolous and some spiteful, but they keep these hidden—which is all one can ask. Well, of course he can ask for more, but he won't get it and he also risks the fragile decorum that obtains for the nonce. (Nonce is a cryptogrammic singularity or a hapax legomenon of an ancient language. Also a sex offender—mostly Australian—as well as a slightly musty word meaning "for the present.")

I could let Vernon know all this, but his mind is elsewhere. And his appetite for learning has waned along with all the others. His curiosity has died. Death, after all, is not instantaneous. One's hair and, I think, fingernails continue to thrive and grow, even in the coffin. They have not yet received the news. In the same way, curiosity has been clever enough to have fled like the rats from an unseaworthy vessel.

How do the rats know? Many people believe that animals have better, keener senses than we do so that among other things they can predict earthquakes. There have been attempts to study this behavior, but it is a difficult experiment to set up because we are less sensitive creatures and have no idea when the quakes will happen; when they do it is too late for us to observe whether the animals predicted it. Anecdotally, lemurs in zoos have been known to shriek fifteen minutes or so before an earthquake. But it is also possible that the lemurs are merely exchanging anecdotes and that their manner of doing so is to shriek.

Interesting, maybe, but not to a dying man. I have tried to work such details into farewell visits to friends of mine whom I have visited as they lay on their deathbeds, but the opportune moment never seems to have presented itself. I like to think that I have shown up and that if they realize this it is probably enough. Some of them seem to be aware, but mostly they want to nap. Is that an authentic desire of the disappearing self, a social maneuver, or merely a side effect of the opiates? Or is it opioids? (And do they have anything to do with Opus the Penguin?) I've never had the chance to ask these questions, either. Often the friend in the bed has closed his eyes and is napping or rehearsing. There is a proposition of Epicurus that says we have nothing to fear from death while we are alive because we are alive, and after we die we have nothing to fear either—because we won't exist. There won't be a we. Not even a teeny-weeny we. (To the tune of "Chiribiribee.")

My mind, as you see, is tap-dancing around the room, shrieking like a lemur (although silently) and I can suppose that his mind is doing the same. I have no evidence for (or against) this idea, but with Dewey—and the others, too—I can have them think whatever I choose. Surely none of them is going to argue with me. Fictional or real, they keep themselves to themselves, as the Brits say.

Dewey? What kind of name is that to give a dying Jew? Altogether too jokey. Dewey, Cheatham, and Howe? Louis, Huey and Dewey? But we may suppose that it could be an Anglicization of *dveykes*, a Talmudic word signifying a communing with God or any experience of religious ecstasy. I like that tension between piety and dopiness, because that's where most of us live most of the time. When we're not napping.

And Vernon? A name from the French, meaning "alder grove." More likely, his parents could have stuck that on him merely because his father had been born in Mt. Vernon—not George Washington's home but the drab city in Westchester County. The appeal of that would be its lack of appeal, but such aporiae are where sophistication often gets us. I had to look up the plural, and there are two. Of course I prefer *aporiae* to *aporias*. It is from the Greek and means a narrow and difficult passage, which was tempting as a title because our dying protagonist is confronting that most difficult of passages. But I resisted: *Vidui, as an English title, is sufficiently recherché. It sounds, misleadingly, like a first-person perfect of a Latin verb. Vidui, viduere, vidui, viduus, meaning anything we like. "To mourn for or be bereaved of" maybe. And not only may be but is. Go ahead and look it up, o ye of little faith. (Mr. Ye, an agnostic Chinese gentlemen, is the proprietor of Ye Old Antique Shop in Camden, Maine, supposing correctly that few of his customers will know what a thorn is.)*

His eyes are closed and his relatives assume he is asleep, but he is feigning because it allows them to talk more freely and him to eavesdrop. Is he curious about what they may say? I have no way of knowing for sure whether or not this is a game, but in his position I'd play whatever games I could. What would be amusing would be to hear what they are saying and marvel at their gullibility, their innocence. Why are they so easily persuaded that he has drifted off and can't hear them? But give them a break. Arnold says something not altogether flattering: "He was always a curmudgeonly guy." Vernon doesn't react. He doesn't mind it and is even pleased, although the past tense is somewhat previous. But is this a time to wrangle about grammar? (Yes! Always!) Anyway, Ruthie also thinks her grandfather is unconscious and she allows herself to agree with her stepfather. As the talk gets more and more frank and earnest, they are more and more persuaded that they can converse in complete candor without any constraint or concern for Vernon's feelings (or Frank's or Ernest's).

It is curious to be there and not there as he has learned from the diapering and it may even be a good way for him to acclimate himself to the freedoms of eternity. "May my death be an atonement for all the errors, iniquities, and willful sins that I have erred, sinned and transgressed before You, and may You grant my share in the Garden of Eden, and grant me the merit to abide in the world to come which is vouchsafed for the righteous." Thus, the prayer. But can one utter such a prayer even at the moment of the commission of sin—assuming that eavesdropping falls into that category? But how can it be sinful when angels eavesdrop all the time, or so we assume? Children, the childlike, and the childish are confident that there are celestial agents of some kind keeping track of us so that everything we do, say, or even think goes on our permanent record in the files of a benevolent, otherworldly STASI.

We may refer to him as the God of our fathers, but perhaps it would be more accurate to call him the God of our children, who have no sense of the absurd and can believe anything. We may be able to remember ourselves as little boys and girls and even to feel some nostalgia for that lost clarity. That kind of belief may not be true, but it is comforting. The desire for it is certainly true, but this is not faith in God but only faith in Faith—the credo of Playdough.

It is logically possible that Vernon actually is asleep and this is his vivid dream. *¿La vida es sueño?* Or is that too cute? (Is cuteness itself evidence of falsity? Do we ever say a thing is too cute to be true? I must try to remember to use that sometime.)

Let us give these apprentice mourners some credit, though. Even if they do say mildly unflattering things about him, they have shown up and they have enough tact to keep themselves from weeping lest their sobs wake him, which would certainly be upsetting. If they are saddened by the prospect of his death, they assume that he, too, must be distraught. (A lost positive? Can one be traught?)

§

It is at this point that we might be expected to provide something in the way of a history, a biography, or at least a description. We probably should have done so before. But does it matter? He no lon-

24

ger looks like the man he was. And his profession, habits, interests, and even his relationships to family and friends have sloughed off or faded into insignificance. They all recede into the past tense in that red shift Hubble described. (Not Carl, the pitcher who once struck out Babe Ruth, Lou Gehrig, Jimmie Foxx, Al Simmons and Joe Cronin in succession, but Edwin, the astronomer—but you knew that.) What history Vernon has left is in the brief flashes that appear in the murk of his illness prompted by some random association, not with the tedious conversation around his bed but rather the ongoing inner prattle of which he has been aware for as long as he can remember. If his identity is anywhere, it is there, in the curious descant to his experience, spontaneous, unstoppable, and unimpeachably authentic.

One aspect of dying that he recognized some time ago and has been simultaneously experiencing and observing, is the diminution of his life's ambit. There came a time when he was no longer willing to undergo the annoyances and discomforts of flying. (What was there there that wasn't here? What was worth the schlepp? People can come to visit me. Or not.) Then he stopped driving and got rid of his car. He'd had a number of near misses and one or two fender-benders and didn't trust himself anymore, at night first and then any time. He was even apprehensive as a passenger, wondering whether they might not be better off if they went slower but unable to say so—which would have been annoying to his driver, often his grandson, who was, after all, doing him a favor. But he was tearing along like Barney Oldfield, because he wanted to get the trip over with as soon as possible. (Or did he just like to drive fast?) Vernon's range shrank and his boundaries continued to contract to exclude other countries, other states, anything more than an hour or so from his house. Map it and you'd get one of those old newspaper illustrations of the changes in the battle lines—with his country clearly losing the war. It was worse than the French, worse than the Poles. A debacle, a rout, a Cannae (Oh, *that* Punic war!) and he withdrew to his walled city to hold out for as long as possible against the besiegers. No, that's extravagant. He did not feel quite so confined at first. It wasn't as if he were under house arrest. He could still venture out occasionally for short trips to the barber or the pharmacy or the podiatrist. But does one *venture* to the pharmacy? That word became less and less of a hyperbole. Still, it was too far to walk and too close for a cab ride. (Or say that it would require an extravagant tip to make the short trip worth the cabbie's while.) Okay, most stuff can be delivered, but that would be—was—a further defeat. ("All hope is not yet lost for the Polish people!" That is the first line of the Polish national anthem, and if you don't believe me, go Google it. Bugle it. Gargle it. Giggle and gag on it!)

Barney Oldfield? My father—and Vernon's, too, I dare say—used Oldfield's name as the personification of speed. In his Blitzen Benz, he set the world speed record in 1910 of 131.724 mph. And for this, the newspapers referred to him as "the speed king." Touching, isn't it? The current land record, Andy Green's, is 763.035. To be candid, I've gone ninety once and that was scary. (Ninety miles per hour, that is, but ninety by itself is frightening.)

So he was housebound and mostly was in the bedroom, the bathroom, and sometimes the kitchen. Then bedridden, but still able to get up to go the toilet or use the sink. And then not. And in the bed, he awaited the further contractions he knew would come. Unable to sit up without using the pull-up bar. And then even with the pull-up bar. Each irreversible step in the declension came with its psychic toll, too, the recognition of yet a further decline. The seven steps of grieving are too optimistic, he found. The first four? Sure. Shock & Denial, Pain & Guilt, Anger & Bargaining, and Depression & Loneliness. Correcterino! But these are supposed to give way to The Upward Turn: Reconstruction, and then Acceptance and Hope. These sometimes fail to appear. Were they ignoring him or were they terrified at the hostile reception they were sure they would get? At best, there was, after each descending step, a numbness, a truce that was better than the grief and rage it had come to replace. Just lying there while his skin wore out and gave way to bedsores, he considered ending it. He could stop eating and drinking and die like a disabled animal in the forest. But that would take considerable time as well as courage and patience. And determination to endure the discomfort. But it was too late for that because there were already tubes in him, delivering nutrition and hydration, the high-sounding words they used because obviously these were not food and water. Not even as metaphors.

§

"A little less conversation, and a little more action please!" It is a line from an Elvis Presley song. A catchy line, it has stuck in my head as an earworm. (Did I envy all the mute lunks who got girls with grunting as their only conversational skill? Only rarely.)

The prospect of some action, any action, is attractive in a novel.

Indeed, there are many readers who think of novels as plots with a few descriptions of places, some dialogue among the characters, and, most important, a satisfying resolution. They are wrong, of course, but not entirely. Even the most sophisticated *littérateur* experiences novels at that primary level, knowing that it is a scaffold for anything else the author may be exploring with us and for us. But what can Vernon do? Levitate and fly through the bedroom window with his ass hanging out of his hospital johnnie? (That might be fun but it would be a different kind of book altogether.) Actually he's in his living room in one of those rented hospital beds that can be cranked to an infinite number of positions and has bars on the sides to keep the occupant from rolling over and falling onto the floor. Or occupants, plural, but seriatim. The hospice people lug these things about for people to die in, the thresholds of death's doors. That would make a macabre TV series, wouldn't it? The episodes would always end the same way with the burly guys putting the bed back into the truck while the credits roll and the lugubrious theme music plays.

It's a living room, yes, but it has been transformed pretty much into a hospital room with all the medical equipment and supplies disposed around the room. The main difference between this and a room on some ward is that this room has a piano in it. But there should be pianos in hospital rooms, too. And pianists in dinner jackets to make rounds every day, taking requests and providing a fragmentary simulacrum of normal life. Or, no, let's not push it too far. Offering a little music, which can be soothing and hath charms to soothe the savage breast. (It's Congreve but is it breast or beast?)

Sure, they have iPods and earphones and radios, but live performances involve the listener more than reproduced, Xeroxed music, taking them out of themselves, where all the patients are dying (*je m'excuse*) to go.

On the piano, which probably doesn't get played anymore, are photographs of relatives in handsome silver frames. The photos should be redundant, because the people in them should be here in person. But let us imagine that each one takes his or her picture home (for the frames, I'm afraid), so that what we have after a while is a gallery of the indifferent, those whom Vernon thought enough of to give them space on the piano but who have not shown any reciprocal concern or affection. (Too elaborate? Never mind.)

But we were about to have some action, even a tiny one, which, for Vernon, would be a laudable achievement. He has been lying there with his eyes closed and his face as still as a death mask of itself. Not moving. Just listening to the blather going on, as the visitors try to maintain a semblance of normality. (Or, as Warren G. Harding would have it, normalcy. And he got elected anyway.) What can Vernon do to engage them? Scare them, perhaps? He has been mulling this over for a while now. His brain has been as busy as ever, and it has always been "curmudgeonly." His repertoire is limited now by his physical disabilities but there must be a way of turning that constraint to his advantage. He could groan, of course, but that would be flat-out lying. That would be the wolf boy who cried and all that could come of it would be that they'd learn to ignore his groans. Not a good idea, especially if there might be real groans later on. Something more subtle then, more equivocal. Or not vocal at all. There is not a flicker of animation on his face and he does not open his eyes, but he moves his left foot an inch or two, laterally. Again. And again.

Let them wonder whether it is a sign of distress. A sign of something, surely. Is it voluntary or involuntary? It could be some benign twitch. Or a kind of palsy. None of them knows and all of them are worried. At this point, any change is likely to be for the worse. He stops. He waits a few moments and then resumes the rhythmic movement of his foot. Will they call the nurse? What will they tell her? That he is moving his foot? A peculiar kind of emergency, requiring nerve to report. (Nerves of the foot? Plantar, perineal, and what else?) None of them wants to appear foolish. Vernon is the foolish one and is enjoying it. He stops. Even more unlikely, someone might now call the nurse to say that he was moving his foot but has stopped. In each one's mind, there must be a struggle between concern and self-regard. Go or not? They discuss it.

"I'd feel like an idiot."

"But it could be important."

"I suppose, but after all, he's dying anyway. And there's nothing they can do about that."

"They can make sure he's comfortable."

"So you go."

"Let's wait a little and see if he does it again."

§

It isn't much of a triumph, but Vernon wasn't expecting a great deal.

He has nonetheless managed to exert for a few moments a degree of control over the world, or at least these people who are looking down at him in his helplessness as if he were some kind of sideshow exhibit. This has been annoying, and he is glad to be able to pay them back, at least momentarily. He twitches the foot again but stops after three or four movements. They see it and resume their discussion about whether cumulatively this merits a trip to the nursing station. They agree, perhaps too readily, that it still isn't worth calling for someone to come.

"I don't think it's serious."

"In his condition, anything can be serious."

"But putting it in another way, nothing can be serious."

Vernon's interest is momentarily piqued. He had never suspected that any of them were gifted in Talmudic disputation. If you say this *(drawing out the vowel and holding as you descend a third from the note on which you started)*...And if this *(same performance)*...But then this *(this time, a monotone staccato)*.

This is what wisdom sounds like. Vernon has reached the point where the words are no longer important but only the tune, the mood, the mode. He developed a sensitivity to this aspect of speech as he was afflicted by presbycusis so that he could hear the melody even if he couldn't make out some of the words. Their discussion is a healthy *mezzo forte* and *affettuoso.* What gives the moment its special savor is that he is enjoying the drama of their situation and is neither remembering something, nor wallowing in his discomforts. He is, for the moment, actively living in the world.

Again? Vernon decides against it. He's had his fun and they will either call for help or not and, frankly, at this point he doesn't much care. Best of all outcomes would be for him to die right here, right now, and let them all feel pangs of guilt that would stay with them not forever probably but for at least a while. When they gather at his graveside in eleven months at the unveiling of his tombstone, the painful thought might recur to one or another of them that maybe they should have called the nurse after all and maybe they were remiss and even in some measure responsible.

Fat chance.

Not a bad name for a cowboy, that. Fat Chance comes riding into town with Slim Pickings. Actually, there was an actor who used that name, Slim Pickens—Louis Burton Lindley, Jr. He mostly played cowboys but he was the guy riding the atomic bomb down as if it were a rodeo bull and waving his hat at the end of *Dr. Strangelove*.

And what does this have to do with the price of turnips in Tuckahoe? Nothing, but such irrelevant thoughts do come to mind and should be represented honestly—dumb things one happens to know and that to a certain extent define him. But would he know that about Lindley? Why not? At least for now, you do.

§

Stupid? Why, yes indeed. But have you never read John Donne's Holy Sonnet with that line John Gunther took for the title of one of his books? *Death Be Not Smart*. Proud, smart, fair, foul, friendly or inimical. None of those things. Does anyone read John Gunther anymore? Or remember who he was? A middlebrow writer who did those Inside books: *Inside the USA, Inside Europe, Inside Africa* and so on. He never got around to Antarctica, but maybe he would have. My version of *Inside Antarctica* would merely point out an unsounded c in there that schoolchildren have to learn about it if they're too lazy to spellcheck. (Is that a verb?)

We all turn out to be citizens of Chelm, which is, in goyish, Gotham (of the three not-so-wise men). The legend is that the Lord sent an angel with a sack full of the souls of fools to distribute around the earth, but the angel tripped, the sack broke, and all those foolish souls escaped and settled in Chelm, a small town that I discover actually exists north of Zamosc and southeast of Lublin, not far from border between Poland and Ukraine. Nowhere is it written that God had a reason for doing such a strange thing, perhaps because it was obvious to the rabbis and storytellers that God doesn't need reasons. (He may not even know what they are. Or to put it another way, the Enlightenment may have been a hoax.)

Without having been summoned, the nurse appears and sends the visitors away. She is here with a small bottle and a dropper and wants to give him his medication, which is best absorbed orally. He has no idea what it's for. The nurse has a fairly good idea, but she isn't volunteering anything unless she is asked. And pressed. One could say that she is keeping it under her hat, except that nurses hardly ever wear hats anymore. Or, no, they're called caps and are adaptations of nuns' headgear. But they don't wear caps either.

She adjusts the bed so that he is halfway sitting up and can swallow more easily. Then she fills the dropper to the prescribed line and moves it to his lips, which he keeps firmly closed. Will she squeeze his nostrils together? Or is that now impermissible?

"Open," she says, cheerfully, going up a third between the syllables. She could be cajoling a small

33

child. "Open" again with the same two notes. Then, in a normal intonation: "The sooner you do, the sooner I'll go away."

With that she reveals a great deal about their relationship. Perhaps in gratitude for his restoration to the status of an adult, he opens. She puts the dropper into his mouth and squeezes the bulb.

To get rid of her, he swallows. He does not believe for a moment that there will be any benefit from this. He knows he is beyond cure, even beyond help. But he is at last in the real world, as none of his visitors seems to be.

They are helping, or pretending to, just as he is pretending to welcome and enjoy their company. Is there ever a time when we can finally abandon pretense and speak truthfully? He has always distrusted language. Those batty Frenchmen, Derrida, de Man, and the other deconstructionists, were onto something, but, as with their revolution, they didn't know when to stop. Language may be slippery but it is all we have binding us together. Ants barely exist as individuals. The unit is the colony, and they even help one another to digest, exchanging the contents of their stomachs in a strange, collective undertaking. Language has that same unimaginable intimacy with each of us contributing a little of his or her being to its ever evolving substance.

My thoughts or Vernon's? Is there a difference? Can there be?

Ordinary men and women recite the prayer, but for novelists there is a special pang when we get to the words "we have imputed falsely."

False imputations are our métier, and if we try to justify ourselves by appealing to some higher truth, we know we are just imputing falsely about another topic.

Vernon's idea, then. But there is a catch to it. The concept of language bringing us together is nothing like what we find in the real world, where we use language to mark social status and separate ourselves. Do you distinguish between "which" and "that"? Are you uncomfortable with the subjunctive? Do you ever give "none" a plural verb? These are points of usage that we make into badges of class. Or weapons to use against others. Years ago, one of Vernon's granddaughters, a freshman at college, misused "disinterested," and he explained to her, for her own good and as a grandparent should do, the difference between that word and "uninterested." A mistake. She was infuriated and felt attacked. That had not been his intention and he was hurt by her accusation and resentment. Decades have elapsed since then, but that is one of the few vivid memories he retains of that young woman, who is not so young now and has improved her manners but is still tetchy. Vernon's hold on even his fictional existence is not particularly firm, but such salient recollections keep him anchored.

That is a most attractive way for a protagonist to behave. He does not impose too much. Among John Gielgud's tips to actors was his advice that they should try not to bump into the furniture. (Or was it Alfred Lunt?) Vernon doesn't do that. He just lies there, breathing, looking, listening, and thinking.

My kind of guy.

§

Shall we let him go? He is not having a good time, but there are moments that aren't so bad. If you are in pain most of the time, any respite is a cause for

35

thanksgiving. The body is nostalgic for how it used to be and what health was like. There are even minuscule moments of…not happiness, but say *bonheur*, which is like happiness but less a state than a fragile, passing condition. A break in the weather that can be a good hour, although it may be mere minutes. His painkillers leave him groggy and less than himself (even his present self), but they do offer temporary respite from *malheur*. He can float for a while in the no-man's land between the pain and the drugs. It is difficult for him not to be grateful for these moments. To whom? Torturers who are on a break?

Early on, he'd hoped he might get a little high from the medicines, but he learned that they don't work that way. The pain uses all their effectiveness and there is nothing left over for fun. Another small disappointment, small only in the sense that his expectations had been modest. Along with the disappointment, there had been a confirmation, because this was the country he had discovered in which the sun rose into a clouded sky every morning to shed its pallid light on a landscape of misfortune in a grave new world.

If life is a gift, then this is part of it. We never asked for anything and we owe the givers—God, our parents, nature? —nothing whatever. If it was a gift, we are entitled to decline it at any time or to dispose of it however and whenever we wish.

If pressed, Vernon would choose another metaphor. God's will, if there is such a thing, is unknowable. But Vernon can understand that he has been dealt a losing hand. (If you stay at the table long enough, you are certain to lose, which is why it is better to own a casino than gamble in one. Just look at the wheel! Zero and double zero? They make it so that even even bets aren't even. The individual numbers pay 36 to one, while the odds are actually 38 to one. *Rien ne va plus.*)

The family are out eating. Or, in Arnold's case, smoking. He is not chastened by the display of medical equipment but then he has managed to ignore his persistent (and annoying) hacking cough for years. By rights, he should be the one in the bed while Vernon is out and about. But "by rights" assumes an altogether different universe, doesn't it? In one of those other dimensions physicists talk about. Or in the dark matter they need to explain certain irksome phenomena of gravity. There are no rights, no wrongs, no goods, no bads, and our ideas of these things are fantasies. Vernon, himself a fantasy, has fantasies. But that ought not to be surprising.

Vernon would be a good name for a frog.

II

Who would have thought any of us would make it to a second chapter—you, me, or Vernon?

Vernon's doctors are surprised. My psychiatrist is probably pleased but he never expresses approval or disapproval, as if life were a poker game, which it may well be. Mathematical skill and nerve are helpful, but they are nothing like a run of good cards to come to the aid even of an un-shrewd and undeserving party. "Now is the time for all good men to come to the aid &c." This has been attributed to Patrick Henry but it is really an exercise devised by Charles E. Weller, a typing instructor. "The quick brown fox jumps over the lazy dog" is a better exercise because it has all twenty-six letters, which makes it a pangram. (These are not easy to do. Or, more accurately, they are difficult if you expect them to make any sense. "Sympathizing would fix Quaker objectives" all but disdains meaning.)

Vernon's eyes are closed but that doesn't mean he is asleep. He knows all too well what the room looks like. His interest is to see other, more interesting *mises en scène*. And as with some stage sets, he can be satisfied with a few salient details from which to extrapolate. He thinks of other bedrooms in which he has lain. All he can recall of some of them with any confidence is where the door was in relation to the bed, but that can be enough. Kitchens, too, are available to him, where the stove was and the sink and the refrigerator. He traveled the routes between them often enough to have worn a path in his mind if not in the tile or linoleum. And then there are places he has never been but has seen often enough in movies to have incorporated them. (Incorporate? That suggests that he brought them into his body. There should be a word that means bringing something into one's mind. Incorticate? Incerebrate? Spellcheck has raised a skeptical eyebrow at both of these, but that can be a kind of compliment.)

So, do we give him some memories or daydreams? I could invent them or lend him some of mine, with the names changed to protect the guilty, but that would be an invasion of his privacy. His secrets are the only possessions he has left even though they are dimmed and tarnished. They don't even matter much, as the prayer makes clear. It isn't your life that flashes before your eyes but ridiculous, brightly colored shards, without the mirrors that would put them into orderly kaleidoscopic patterns. Just random rubble of various colors. But it's yours, although you are about to disappear and ownership means less than it used to. Unless, like Proudhon, you think that all property is theft, inventing dreams to substitute for his, a kind of property, would also be theft. (Did Jung think that?) Thoughts, affections preferences, and fears are all theft, too. Individuation itself is theft. Ask the ants.

§

On Yom Kippur, we have prayers that really are confessions of sins. The prayer that lists them rolls on in a rhythm like that of a heartbeat or breathing and we recite them, beating our chests. They are various and vivid:

> For the sin which we have committed before You by false denial and lying.
> And for the sin which we have committed before You by a bribe-taking or a bribe-giving hand.
> For the sin which we have committed before You by scoffing.
> And for the sin which we have committed before You by evil talk.
> For the sin which we have committed before You in business dealings.
> And for the sin which we have committed before You by eating and drinking.
> For the sin which we have committed before You by taking or giving interest and by usury.
> And for the sin which we have committed before You by a haughty demeanor.
> For the sin which we have committed before You by the prattle of our lips.
> And for the sin which we have committed before You by a glance of the eye.
> For the sin which we have committed before You with proud looks.
> And for the sin which we have committed before You with impudence.
> For all these, God of pardon, pardon us, forgive us, atone for us.

> For the sin which we have committed before You by casting off the yoke of Heaven.
> And for the sin which we have committed before You in passing judgment.
> For the sin which we have committed before You by scheming against a fellowman.

And for the sin which we have committed
before You by a begrudging eye.
    For the sin which we have committed before
You by frivolity.
    And for the sin which we have committed
before You by obduracy.
    For the sin which we have committed before
You by running to do evil.
    And for the sin which we have committed
before You by tale bearing.
    For the sin which we have committed before
You by swearing in vain.
    And for the sin which we have committed
before You by causeless hatred.
    For the sin which we have committed before
You by embezzlement.
    And for the sin which we have committed
before You by a confused heart.
    For all these, God of pardon, pardon us, for-
give us, atone for us.

Tough stuff, that. Prattle and frivolity are sins? A
confused heart is a sin? A glance? A begrudging eye?
Neither Vernon's prospects nor mine are very bright.
    Either God is very stern or else it was the rabbis
who were speaking for him when they wrote this list.
Were they joking with us, cackling until the saliva ran
down their luxurious beards? Who figured out that
running toward a sin might, in itself, be sinful?
    It can't be a mere prank. I think it is a slightly
less graceful version of the other, mysterious but
altogether persuasive sin—casting off the yoke of
Heaven. I can offer rational objections to that but I
can't deny that it resonates. As between resonation
and ratiocination, which do we trust? The list in the

Vidui is less extensive than the Yom Kippur prayer but still it is traditionally recited with the same beating of the chest.

Granted, it is unlikely that these august sages were pulling our legs, but if an idea challenges belief, that is not exactly evidence against it.

Credo quia absurdum, as Tertullian never said. It is a misquote, a collectively mistaken attribution that has spread widely enough to displace the truth. The truth? I'd vote at this point for the misquote. (Miss Quote wins; Miss Truth is only the runner-up, the best of the losers, and her prize is smaller.)

§

Michel Butor died this week. The frog novelist, one of those *nouveau roman* guys. (Heigh ho, said Rowley!) Butor's obit included a line he is alleged to have written (but the allegation could be wrong: the words could be different and their author somebody else). Anyway: "Every written word is a victory over Death."

From the recesses of that study house of the laughing rabbis, there comes a faint echo that is the only possible comment. Languages die. Etruscan, for instance. And the immortality of the written word is an obviously false and sentimental idea. Do business letters live forever? "Please remit!" stamped on a Babylonian bill? In any event, Butor is as dead as any of the others on the obituary page. Dead as a doornail, as Shakespeare said, or maybe it was Patrick Henry. No, William Langland. Really. (Come to think of it, what are doornails?) Of course it is possible to argue that Butor was kidding. If you have a finely enough honed sense of humor and are spiritually tough enough, all literature is kidding. (Do you go to performances of *King Lear* mainly to see whether the old king will drop Cordelia in the last act? That is what the actor playing Lear is worrying about. Cordelia, too, I suppose, because elderly actors like to do Lear and the actresses don't want to be dropped on their asses.)

What I'm driving at is that belief doesn't depend on plausibility but rather defies it. The less likely a proposition is, the more probable it is. As a young man, I rejected the looniness of Judaism, but that is what now attracts me to it as a reasonable response to a loony world. The rationality of irrationality is a concept economists find useful. Also dermatologists. (See: The Rationality of Irrationality in Eczema by Thomas Ruzicka, MD, which would make an appealing coffee-table book.)

And Vernon's view? Who knows? He's lying there with his eyes closed, breathing regularly and, while he might be sleeping, he can be thinking whatever he wants. (Or we want.) He appears to be comfortable. At least his foot is not twitching. Possibly, he is thinking about his visitors. Some of them will be upset for a while when he expires, but of course they will be the wrong ones. In any sensible apportionment of grief, it would be the ones who cared least or who didn't even like him, who would be most grief-stricken as they regret not only his death but their indifference to him during his lifetime and their thoughtlessness, which can no longer be remedied. The ones who loved him deserve to feel no more than a comfortable sadness that tints their acceptance.

Is there a way to contrive such a complicated arrangement? It is too much to think about. He lets it go and considers instead the curious phenomenon of regret. Does it ever do any good or is it merely an elaborate piece of self-indulgence? In theory, it might prompt someone to reconsider his actions and perhaps to amend his behavior so as to avoid such lapses in the future. In practice, however, that doesn't happen very often. There may be solemn resolutions, of course, but they seldom last. We tend to return to whatever was in our character. The discomfort of regret fades, as do the ambitions to improve. An exquisite sensibility may find that, too, regrettable, but this is only aesthetics, floral arrangements at an altar at which this *Feinschmecker* of morality never intends to pray. For old men who are more realistic or at least inured to their imperfections and those of the world, the probability of reform is even lower. Crying over spilt milk is not only a strange thing to do but it makes the milk salty so the cat is puzzled as he laps it up.

You remember the defiance of the Edith Piaf song's declaration, *"Je ne regrette rien."* You can look at its refusal as sophistication. Or honesty.

She tells us that she knows and therefore won't apologize for who she is. She is, in other words, a grown-up. This leads us back to the Vidui, which, as I read it, doesn't apologize so much as it offers an accounting.

I used to think that Catholics were sensible, letting men and women act however they pleased but assuring them of a place in heaven if they confessed at the end and had a good death. A terrific deal that Protestants thought was too good to be true. But Jews have it, too. There is another prayer in the liturgy of the High Holidays, the *Unesanneh Tokef,* that tells us that God is:

hard to anger and easy to appease,

44

for You do not wish the death of one deserv-
ing death,

but that he repent from his way and live.

Until the day of his death You await him;

if he repents You will accept him immediately.

It is true that You are their Creator and You
know their inclination, for they are flesh and
blood. A man's origin is from dust

and his destiny is back to dust.

At risk of his life he earns his bread;

he is likened to a broken shard, withering
grass,

a fading flower, a passing shade, a dissipating
cloud,

a blowing wind, flying dust, and a fleeting
dream.

The theology is pleasant, but it is the poetry that
carries authority.

And beckons. It distracts us from thoughts of
death, posing an attractive alternative that is not at
all sappy. One might say the same thing of the great
tradition of funeral music, the requiems of Mozart,
Verdi, Berlioz, Fauré, and the others that overwhelm
us, or, more precisely, overwhelm our reason. You
can try to make fun of them and translate the words
to nonsense (the D. A.'s Era) but their majesty is impossible to diminish.

[But who would do such a stupid thing? It's a
kind of vandalism, isn't it? Well, no, not necessarily. It can be a protest against artistic bullying. I am
not certain but I think it was Benjamin Britten who
referred sometimes to Handel's Honolulu Chorus—
which changes drastically if you substitute the name

of the Hawaiian city for "Hallelujah." Or the Duchamp's Mona Lisa with the mustache and goatee and the letters "L.H.O.O.Q. inscribed below. The letters don't spell anything but if you pronounce them in the French manner, they make a homonym for *She itches in her cunt.* Madonna mia!]

The alternative to esthetic admiration and belief, meanwhile, is grim. The impending condition of non-being is not only unpleasant but difficult to think about and philosophically challenging because non-being cannot have attributes. Can there be a bright not-green? Can there be a silence in b flat? Can there be a location for nothingness? Better yet, is there some non-world of dark matter in which adjectives float about looking for the nouns they would need in order to signify anything?

There are no easy answers to these questions but for that very reason they are enchanting as they bring back the wonder he felt long ago as a small boy, asking in wide-eyed ignorance why the sky was blue. They told him, but he has of course forgotten. Invincible ignorance is a category in Catholic theology, where it can be a good thing. Someone who is invincibly ignorant has an excuse so that his sins cannot be mortal. (Are immortal sins what we really want? Those would be the sins of angels, or sins that are punished, yea, unto the seventh generation. [Yay, way to go, seventh generation!])

§

The nurse comes in to change his diaper and clean him up. He tells himself that this is part of her job and she must have known it would be when she enrolled in nursing school. How much worse is it than mucking out stables? (Lots, because horseshit smells much less bad than our own.) But this is none of his business, even though it is his business that she's cleaning up. The difficult part for her, he supposes, is in not making faces or showing disgust in any way. Bowel movements. Movements of the bowels. Bowels of the earth. Those would be earthquakes, which are also disagreeable. Or *désagréable*. It sound less disagreeable in French with those cute, acutes, but does that make it less accurate? Would it be more grave with graves? Peut-être. (One peut-être, two peut-être, three peut-être, four! *Un, deux, trois* cats sank.)

Vernon takes a slight satisfaction from the idea of bowel movements of the earth. It is a silly but not a stupid thought. What pleases him, mostly, is that he has never said these words in this order before. It is a novelty to him and, not inconceivably, to the language itself. Doctors and nurses feel pulses, listen for heartbeats, hold mirrors up to the mouth to detect respiration (or is that only in movies?) but the ability to make jokes, even feeble ones, is evidence of life— even a feeble one, with rough breathing and requiring a diaeresis machine.

He has been napping, which, on a pediatric ward would be kidnapping. (Oh, come on!) Naps are his primary occupation these days. Each of them is a rehearsal—a *répétition*—of dying, except that that when these run-throughs end he wakes up. They are like a suicide he can take back. So far, anyway. And he will keep on doing this until he gets it right! It is like practicing a musical instrument to achieve that adequate level that is only the beginning of the real work.

As the nurse turns to leave with her malodorous laundry in a plastic sack emblazoned with the name of the hospice (Who steals plastic sacks, empty or

47

full? Or are these a kind of advertisement?), he says, "Tell them I'm sleeping." This is a sentence that can never be true. To say it, then, or even perhaps to think it is to commit one of the sins in that long list. Can invincible intelligence also be a get-out-of-jail-free ticket? It isn't that he doesn't want to see any of his visitors, or suffer them all staring at him, but that he'd rather be alone with his own thoughts that are more interesting. At least for a while. Indeed, what he will miss most (if there is a he and it is capable of missing anything) would be this almost unending lo-gopoetic play of memory and association. It will, of course, come to an end, but as M. Butor should have realized, immortality is not necessarily a good thing. The immortal gods can never be serious because they cannot die. Because men die, what they do and say is definitive and important. Whatever passes away is all the more precious for that.

§

A week earlier, in the hospital:

Dr. Hau comes to pay a visit. He is the palliative care doctor attached to the hospice. Vernon can't help translating his name into Doc Hau, as in the concentration camp, but he has kept this to himself on the off chance that the good doctor may be able to help him in some small way. Surely, he won't be doing any harm. Not intentionally, anyway.

But as it turns out unintentional harm is as bad as any other kind, and maybe even worse, arising as it does from stupidity, for which there is no known cure. Hau brings with him a template from the Stanford Friends and Family Letters Project. (Yes, there is such a thing. You doubt me? Ask yourselves if I am likely to have made it up.) The template is designed to enable communication between the dying patient and his/her survivors, and "help people complete seven life review tasks: acknowledging important people in our lives; remembering treasured moments; apologizing to those we may have hurt; forgiving those who have hurt us; and saying 'thank you,' 'I love you' and 'goodbye.' " Who can object to that? No one is obliged to participate, and for those who are not comfortable with the undertaking a simple "No, thank you" is sufficient. Vernon, however, is distressed, as I would be, too, although that would follow (or precede). The purpose of the template is to help the inarticulate express themselves, but their true selves are inarticulate. Any expression is therefore untrue and inauthentic, even a betrayal of the deficiencies that have been important parts of their lives. The recipients, too, may be inarticulate but unless they are altogether dense they will recognize the mechanical contrivance of the missive. These poor bastards should be allowed to say goodbye in their own clumsy way, smiling, waving, grunting, maybe blowing a kiss. Or a Bronx Cheer. Whatever they have picked up from the movies or TV and included in their limited repertoire.

[To be fair, I should declare that I received an email from Dr. V. J. Periyakoil, the director of the Family and Letters project saying:

> A person should only write what is true and aligns deeply with their held values. People can choose to complete some or all of the seven common tasks. There is no mandate to complete all seven tasks. If inclined and truly able to forgive people who have hurt us, we can choose to do so.

I happen to believe that an unpleasant event links two people together just as much as a pleasant and loving event links us to others. One might even argue that the intensity of emotion invoked by unpleasant events is higher and binds us tighter to others involved in the unpleasantness. By forgiving, sometimes, it is possible to let go of our attachment to the unpleasant event, thereby extricating ourselves from the specific incident(s) and reinvesting the energy in something more positive.

Brava! Up until the end, I agree entirely. It is her bias toward positivity that raises my eyebrow slightly, if not my hackles, although we should probably make allowances. She's a doctor, after all, and they are by disposition and training inclined toward meliorism.]

Meanwhile, and not entirely coincidentally, Vernon asks himself if he wants to forgive those who have offended him or have been rude or ungrateful? Does death turn us all into Pollyannas? When the noisy children come unto me, aren't they the ones who should suffer rather than me? Are all the judgments we made when we were healthy and of sound mind (comparatively) to be gainsaid by a Procrustean form from a committee of doctors who have never met us? Do our years of lived experience count for nothing? Is it medically ethical for them to prescribe for patients they have never seen? These may be over-the-counter offerings, but they are linguistic opioids, which are worse.

The Stanford people may be doctors and social workers of some culture and refinement but they are dealing with patients who believe in pop songs, sitcoms, and movies with reliably happy endings after an hour or so of amusing misunderstanding. Even if they don't know anything, they deserve to be comforted. The palliative care people have to take them as they come and work with them however they can. I know all that, but still…

"You don't have to follow it exactly," Dachau explains, trying not to take Vernon's objections personally. "It's supposed to be at most a series of suggestions."

But Vernon directs the doctor's attention to the first paragraph and says, "What bovine ordure is this?" The crap is 'I realize that my illness may be causing you some distress. You are working hard to support me and care for me in addition to all the other roles and responsibilities you have. Let me start by saying that I am very grateful to you for your loving care and concern. Your support is helping me cope with my illness.'

"That's a bit self-serving, is it not? And should I be grateful? Are these health care professionals doing it for me or for themselves? This is their job. They get paid, some of them far too much. Are the care and concern I get supposed to make up for all their profession's limitations? Even if I were grateful to some of them, it wouldn't be to 'all,' would it? My body is shot but my mind still works. This is just presumptuous."

Dachau tries to defend himself. "These are only general suggestions," he says again, with the frustration of a wizard whose magic spell isn't working.

Vernon pauses. Is it worth answering him? "I'm not a general; I'm a private," he mutters at last, not so much for the doctor as because he can't resist the formulation. "Anything that applies to everybody actually applies to no one."

The doctor, exasperated, uses his fallback line: "I'll leave it for you to think about."

"I've done thinking about it. It's not complicated.

Throw it out. Or I'll have the nurse do it. And I'll have her throw you out, too. Just because you aren't dying yet doesn't mean that you're smarter than I am. All I want from you is renewals on the pain medications. Two of my grandsons are lawyers and, if need be, I'll sic them on you like a pair of junkyard dogs. You got that? Concentrate on it." Much of this he says after Hau has left the room, so it is less rude than it could have been.

(Why had Vernon not wanted to be rude? Because it can be fun to feign civility, a game he has played many times, and for which he doesn't get many opportunities these days.)

There is more he could have said of course. There always is. It crosses his mind that deathbed testimony is not treated as hearsay evidence but is generally given credence in judicial proceedings. Why would a dying person lie, after all? (Lots of reasons, actually.) To elicit fraudulent statements from those about to quit this world would then seem particularly heinous. At the same moment, however, it also crosses his mind that it isn't worth his energy or time to pursue this. Hau is altogether convinced of the rightness—even the righteousness—of what he is trying to do.

§

Now that a week has passed—a lifetime, nearly—Vernon is still troubled by the doctor's clumsiness. Not deeply troubled but, say, ruffled. Disgruntled. (Can one be gruntled?) It has always been a habit of his to hang onto these things and hold grudges longer than most reasonable people would. But this is not merely baggage: it is who he is. If this is a failing, it will remedy itself soon enough.

52

His final instructions are in an envelope in the top desk drawer. Not sealed. A frugal fellow, he didn't want to waste an envelope if he changed his mind about anything. For instance, years ago, he had thought it would be a good idea to leave his body to a medical school so that students could learn anatomy from it. A generous action, it would cost him nothing. And it would have been a suitably brusque response to a body that had failed him. Let them hack it to pieces. Let them fling his organs around the room. But one of his granddaughters, a doctor, told him that this fantasy was not so far-fetched and that she hated the idea. She begged him not to do it. The way they treat the bodies, she said, was "gross," because that was how they tried to distance themselves and overcome the guilt they felt about what they were doing. It was understandable but not pretty. She would be uncomfortable thinking about him. "Please!" she had implored. "For my sake." And he had agreed.

So, cremation, which isn't pretty either but is quicker. They could throw his ashes into Nantucket Sound. (Is that legal? Would they do it anyway?) And no funeral. He doesn't believe in them. He doesn't like the prospect of people he didn't much care for or who had behaved badly to him taking credit for their charade of piety just for having shown up. Meanwhile those he liked or loved and who had behaved well toward him would not find much solace in the ceremony. Real grief is not so easily assuaged. He would not, therefore, be depriving anyone of comfort if they indulged his whim.

Of course, he could have them hold a funeral at which someone read a Family Letter he could write, telling them all what he really thought of them. But

there would be no point unless he were there to observe. The prospect of death may not be a cheerful
one but it does seem to offer a surcease of *tsuris*. If
you don't exist anymore, you can't be angry and you
can't care. Ray's Ipsa Loquitur (it's a bar where Lati-
nists hang out). Affronts, unkindnesses, and resent-
ments legitimate or not all dissolve or float away with
the smoke from the crematorium chimney. Buddhist
in a way. No more desires or emotions of any kind.
Nirvana, or something like it. Sweetness, bitterness,
gentleness and curmudgeonliness no longer exist.
"Cured, cured, you're all cured; go and sin no more,"
Vernon had often said, using the line as a joke. "Put
your hand on the radio and your pain will be gone!"
Back in the days when radios had tubes that made
them warm, certain kinds of arthritic pain could actually diminish from the heat and the hope.

He had not liked the idea of a memorial service
either, with the twaddle the speakers would spout.
Could he comfortably contemplate a rabbi, a perfect
stranger, who would be working from his notes of a
couple of brief conversations…and a template? Hau
do you do? It is the doctor again, but in a tallit instead
of a white coat with his name embroidered on it, the
popinjay who keeps popping up. On all other nights,
we eat both leavened bread and unleavened bread,
but on this night we eat only bitter herbs and horseshit, which turns out to be the blue-plate special, sufficient unto the day.

It would not be impossible, though, even in our
imperfect world, for those who were smart, or sane,
or merely awake, to discern who was speaking the
truth (or something near it) and who was defiling language itself with their betrayals of reality. If there
were a God, there would be an automatic mechanism

dispensing justice to each and all who spoke falsely with the prattle of their lips and a haughty demeanor. But can he bring himself to believe that? Or even imagine it? Any lie would be betrayed by the blast of a jeering horn, as in T. or C.

But no such luck. They would all get together at the memorial service and lie to each other, and none would be the wiser. (A wink is as good as a nod to a blind horse.) They would continue in their ignorant wickedness, just as they deserved. No mercy for the wicked. *Non? Merci! Merci d'hautes.*

Does he really think any of this or is he only trying it on like a jacket off the rack to see whether it fits. Will a little tailoring help?

The kettle of vultures have tired of flying around in circles in the dining room and they want to come in again to perch around him and hold him with their glittering eyes. "Why not?" he says to the nurse. That's what a Buddhist would say, isn't it? Even a novice? A budding Buddhist. Whine not. They come straggling in, preening their feathers, and perch in the places they had before. They seem to be waiting for him to say something that passes for wisdom: "Life is not a fountain," or "To thine own self be true." But better than that he says, "Amuse me, someone." And they are all stricken dumb, as he was sure they would be.

§

This is how he relaxes, with his mind skittering like a waterbug—or water strider, or Jesus bug—able to walk on water, darting along the surface tension on its long, hydrofuge legs. The process is rather like the taxiing of a plane before takeoff, crossing runway after runway, making apparently random turns, and

55

then, with an increase in the engine's sound, advancing fast enough to leave the earth and ascend into the mild blue yonder.

But planes don't really taxi, do they? Have you ever stood out on a runway, briefcase in one hand while trying to flag a plane with the other? As a rule planes don't stop. Or have taximeters. The origin for this use is most likely from the early twentieth-century phrase about how "the only way to get this bus in the air is by taxi." Not altogether satisfying, is it? But better than nothing.

This is the criterion people should use who are contemplating suicide: is this better than nothing? If the answer is in the negative, you should have it developed. (There's a metaphor that will be dying eventually because nobody uses film anymore.) Happiness is when life is good and the prospect is that it will keep getting better. Misery is the opposite, when conditions are intolerable and appear to be getting even worse. This is a distressing thought for Vernon, but he has simplified the question and now only asks whether he can still stand it, and for how long? It, being existence. (Move over Clara Bow, for each one of us is an "it girl.")

But there is also the expletive *it*. It is there. There it is. He prides himself on remembering some of the rules about expletives and how to distinguish them from referentials. Expletives are never accented. It is one of those things you know but don't know you know. The grammar changes, depending on whether or not you stress the first word. Which is lovely.

(As long as there are still occasions to remark on the loveliness of anything, there is a certain—or uncertain? —value to life.)

He feels a moment of sadness, not for himself so

much as for the jumble of information in his brain that will be lost when he dies. Each factoid, each fleeting thought is like one of those quick sketches Picasso used to do at the beach with a stick in the wet sand, so that people could watch, helpless and sad, as the tide rolled in to obliterate it.

§

"What do you want? Jokes?" one of his grandsons asks, grinning. The question itself is probably a joke. Its intention was almost certainly kindly—to break the silence while it was still frangible. Vernon is pleased by the young man's initiative. He has long ago given up on the sentimental notion that some part of him will survive in his children and their children, not just in genes and chromosomes but in taste and character. (Anyway, one is the source of only an eighth of a grandchild's genes.) He also came to realize that this familial similitude he had been imagining might not necessarily be a good thing—for him (he'll be dead) or them. There are surely other ways to live than he has contrived for himself and there is at least a hope that some of them might do better, achieve more, or just be happier.

His wishes don't matter. He doesn't believe that anyone has any choices anyway. People will do what they do, playing their hands as well as they can with an incomplete deck and ignorant of the odds and even the rules of the game.

To consider the world and not feel offended is irrational. The Gnostics had the right idea—that existence itself was tainted. Better to be an unrealized idea, or less even than that, than to tolerate the wretchedness that lies at the heart of being. Angels, for instance, don't pee, don't shit, don't fart, don't spit. They don't have to blink. Or even breathe, probably. Their secret? They are figments.

The Gnostics believed that the devil made the world—or a demiurge in a devil costume. (Trick or treat!) That would explain the awfulness of things. Existence itself may be an affront to God. The best we can hope for is to get out of it, leave it behind, and settle in to the Brownian motion of mindless bits of matter that would be fun if we (or they) were aware of it. Are Buddhists in the same ballpark as Gnostics? And do these teams have designated hitters or do the pitchers come to bat?

According to the Gospel of Philip, one of the Gnostic texts, "Jesus came to crucify the world." Mysterious but attractive. Or attractive because it is mysterious.

All that in an instant? Of course. The trouble with trying to follow someone's thoughts is that you have to do it in words, which slow you down.

Without them, the neurons fire away at amazing speed (except that they are not, themselves amazed, which is why we don't realize what's happening).

"Was that the joke?" Vernon asks his grandson.

"Not if you didn't think so," Jacob-never-Jake replies.

"No, no. But *that* was a joke," Vernon answers, pokerfaced.

Jokes, not that one in particular but that they are still possible, are reassuring. Funny.

§

He allows himself a short, gentle chuckle, which turns out to have been unwise, for it changes almost

58

immediately to a racking cough, painful and yet insufficiently powerful to bring up the phlegm that has accumulated in his bronchi. The cough persists long enough to frighten some of his relatives, one of whom goes to fetch the nurse. She appears forthwith (one of the advantages of private-duty nurses), shoos everyone out of the room again, and puts the respirator tube past his tongue and a little way down his throat, managing to do so without making him gag. She is able to extract a fair amount of phlegm and clear his airways. She offers him some water. He accepts and she brings him a Sippy Cup full of ice water. He takes a few small sippies. The nurse looks down at him and decides that his hair is disarranged enough to require attention. Without asking, she runs a comb through it and Vernon is pleased not to have been asked and not to have had to ask.

"Thank you," he says. He has blanked on her name. Internally, he thinks of her as Charlotte Rampling, not because she looks anything like the actress but because he once had a terrible time trying to recall Rampling's name. He imagined himself putting little slips of paper in all his pockets with her name on them so it would always be available. But supposing he were hit by a bus, what would the ER people think? So he didn't do it, but Rampling became the X that stood for anything he was unable to remember, a not particularly helpful stratagem. So he thought of the nurse as Charlotte but he couldn't use that to address her. Explaining would be too tedious.

Decades earlier, he had thought of all nurses as Jane, from *Jane Amor, Space Nurse*, a soft-core porn novel he had seen on a table of sale books. It was bizarre enough so that he had no trouble remembering it. Indeed, he was unable to forget it. But he doesn't

have to rely on it anymore. Charlotte. Not-Rampling!
All right, then Charlotte Mousse. Or Charlotte Russe.
(Are they the same thing?) O Mistress Mousse are
you within? Heigh ho said Charlotte Rampling.

"Shall I call them back in?"

He sighs through his nicely cleared bronchi and
manages a Zeus-like affirmative nod.

So why would dying alone be such a bad thing? Quieter that way and with fewer distractions. In the last moments of your life, you ought to be paying attention. Everyone else, everything else is like some of the luggage of years ago on ocean liners with the proud label, "Not wanted on voyage." Just as long as you are not in pain, the solitude would be comfortable—and maybe even a foretaste of the nothingness that is to come.

Just to lie there and be aware of your breathing and hear that pianissimo pounding in the blood vessel in the ear that comes from the beating of your heart. Almost certainly, you won't be aware of their cessation, awareness itself having been simultaneously extinguished. The mind is not designed to imagine such things, because there can never be an occasion for it to do so.

§

Later. The visitors have returned to their homes, hotel rooms, or convertible sofas in the living rooms of hospitable relatives. The only one left is Jacob-not-Jake, who may not be able to do anything Nurse Charlotte can't do better or, indeed, anything at all useful. But there was a discussion—there must have been—about how it would look (to whom?) if they all left. Jacob volunteered and Vernon can see him lying on the couch covered by an afghan. He may or may not be asleep. Actually, Vernon is pleased that he is there because he is one of the grandchildren Vernon actually likes. A good kid, although at 28 (already?) not really a kid anymore.

The prospect of their having any real conversation is dim, but because he is there on the sofa, the possibility is there with him. Between them. A connection, albeit tenuous.

If he were awake, what would they talk about? How could they say in a brief time all that needed to be said? Or rather ask how they could even try without embarrassing each other? Maybe that Stanford letters project isn't so stupid? But, yes, of course it is! Better to have an honest, earnest, even uncomfortable silence than a series of unpersuasive fictions that Jacob would never forget and that he, Vernon, would remember for the rest of his life—a week? A few days?

Call out to him? Ask if he is sleeping? Vernon thinks better of it, not wishing to be a bother. Or to frighten him. He stares at the body under the afghan, trying to observe any movement. Perhaps the slight weight of his gaze will have an effect and Jacob will wake. But there is another way to solve the problem. He makes a noise, something between a groan and a sigh, not too loud and with no note in it of pain or distress.

Almost immediately, "Grandpa?"

"Yes," he says. "Who else would it be?"

"Are you okay? Do you need anything?"

"No, I'm fine. Thanks for asking."

"That's what I'm here for." And then, a beat later, "I'm glad to be here."

"I know," Vernon says, very softly, almost as if he were talking to himself and Jacob were merely eavesdropping. Neither of them speaks for a while. Thirty seconds, say, which is quite a long time in actuality. Then Vernon says, "We ought to have a lot to say to each other. But I can't think what it would be."

"It isn't necessary, is it?" A pause, and then, "We have talked before, so the question is what more do we have to say?"

"A good way to put it," Vernon says. "I was worried that you might ask me something stupid, like 'Did you like your life?'"

"Only as a set-up, so you could say, 'Compared to what?'"

It is a luxury Vernon has often enjoyed with Jacob—not having to calculate what he says or think how it might be misinterpreted. He has had no need to edit or censor himself. Not because Jacob is better than the other grandchildren (although it does sometimes seem that way) but just randomly their minds meshed easily. Neither one of them had to exert effort. It is a gift they shared and, like all gifts, was unearned.

§

Deeply moving. Or is it an author's trick by which he can avoid thinking up and writing down their dialogue? The specific words don't make any difference anyway. We're imaging them and you can invent their conversation as well as I. By this time, we have come to a tacit agreement (which doesn't have any words

63

either). What we do here we do together. Or do we? Or Dewey? One need not feign the factual to tell the truth. The invented dialogue would only be an encumbrance. What was most persuasive in the foregoing, I think, were the Pinter's *pittoresque* pauses, all those virtuoso rests and crochets with which he embellished his actors' lines. Their purpose was to focus the attention of the audience. To hone it as a butcher hones his knives with the sharpening steel. Honing a boning knife on a sharpening stone? It happens, I should expect, and not infrequently.

Woolgathering of this kind will sooner or later get spun and woven to provide the material for a shroud, although linen is the more usual fabric, perhaps because it is less vulnerable to moths. (Do moths often get into coffins?) And if I remember correctly, we are enjoined from wearing linen and wool together, the point being that the prohibition is pointless. Those laughing rabbis again? A whole study-house full of Jackie Masons?

The question, *messieurs-dames*, is whether these are Vernon's random thoughts or mine pretending to be his. A close reading (as by the myopic) might suggest that Vernon is clinging to life by a thread and is still here but just barely. We met him when he was, as the poet-obstetricians say, crowning. From that primitive paranomasia (v. Dewey) came this homunculus that has quickened, lived, quickly aged, and already reached the end of his span. And his grandson Jacob-not-Jake. A generic patriarchal name. These appear informally sometimes as Abe, Ike, and Jake, but then they sound like the owners of a deli or an army-navy store.

Actually, Jacob's mother once told him that Jake sounded like a beer-truck driver's helper. This assumes some actuality somewhere, but it would be difficult to avoid entirely, wouldn't it? *Donnez-moi un fracture!* (That's not at all an actual phrase, but its four words, now that they have been written down, do have a faint actuality after all.)

It is by such threads, gossamer but with considerable tensile strength, that Vernon's life hangs over the abominable abyss. An intelligent fellow, he has a sense of the precariousness of his situation but he doesn't worry about it much because he has given up on life. It was the only sensible thing to do when life had given up on him. What will he miss? Would it be amiss to do so? But what could he miss if there were a he to miss things? Jacob, for instance? Yes, but he is realistic enough to admit the likelihood of a young man outliving his parents and the near inevitability of his outliving his grandparents. The most difficult part of parenting is learning how to let go. Grandparents, too, can find it stressful even though they have had practice.

There is a Philip Roth novel called *Letting Go* about the mess young people can make of their love lives. A comedy, really, except that Roth takes it all (gives it all) very seriously. Maybe that's the joke. Anyway, the real dramas that almost all of us go through are about parents letting go of their children and vice versa. Lovers letting go of each other. Or the sick and elderly letting go of the world. When Roth grows up (*Letting Go* is a very early novel) he learns this. And his books get better. Wiser.

Vernon knows enough not to be greedy. He has watched Jacob grow up, not so closely as he might have liked but enough to have a clear idea about the child, the youth and then the young man. And from what he knows, he can project and at least roughly imagine the shape of a future for him. That's enough, isn't it? Again, the details are unimportant. What counts is character and intelligence. And taste, maybe? And a sense of humor.

There have been other losses; many of his friends have dropped away. They have not dropped him but have just dropped. Dead. You get old enough and it happens more and more frequently. The conventional wisdom is that you should make new, younger friends, but forming friendships becomes more difficult, because younger people seem not to know anything and to care about the wrong things The affectionate *mon vieux* acknowledges a parity of experience that coevals find in one another. Even intelligent young people lack the mellowness distillers try for as they store their whiskey in barrels to age it. But there is a limit. At eighteen years, Scotch is at is peak, but after that it begins to get grumpy. The twenty-one year old stuff is more expensive but doesn't go down so well.

Vernon realizes that one of the reasons for his inability to make new friendships is laziness, which is his fault. But caution is also a factor, and for that he cannot blame himself. It may be better to have loved and lost than never to have loved at all, but it is also more strenuous and often painful.

§

"Do you need anything? Do you want anything?"

"Need? No. Want? Some Chinese food would be nice, but don't run out to get any. I'd only be able to eat a tiny bit and I probably wouldn't be able to keep that down anyway. So it would be depressing."

After a moment's thought, Jacob says, "Wanting

it is better than having it and being disappointed."

"That's life," he says. "Or most of it." Odd how their thoughts are congruent.

"Are you joking? Or not?" his grandson asks.

"Yes."

Jacob has crossed the room and is now standing beside his grandfather's bed. He doesn't say anything but he puts his hand lightly on Vernon's forearm, a metonymic hug. Or would it be synecdochical? (Or synecdochal? Were there anarcho-synecdochalists?) The love that dare not speak its name because it doesn't know it. Jacob stands there without moving, breathing quietly, and looking down at his grandfather until he has determined, from a slowing of the breathing, that the old man is asleep again. Carefully, he removes his hand. There is no discernable reaction. He pads back across the room to lie down on the sofa. No way to know if his grandfather was comforted by this gesture, but Jacob was and he supposes that there might have been a concinnity of their feelings. (Is concinnity a sin that two or more people commit together?)

IV

He has been sleeping. He must have been because he has woken up. Or rather he has left the
dream he was having to return to the nightmare of
his sickbed. The "mare" in nightmare comes from
the Middle Dutch and also appears in the French
"cauchemar." Vernon's dream was not particularly
cauchemardesque but it was unsettling. He was on the
floor, picking fleas off the belly of an old dog. (It
was unclear which dog. He has had several during
his lifetime.) What was most vivid was his feeling of
frustration as he chased the tiny insects across the
white skin of the animal's abdomen and they raced
to safety in the forest of hair in which they could
hide. Only rarely did he manage to seize one of
them and crush its carapace between the nails of his
index finger and thumb. That deeply satisfying pop.

But of all the shreds and patches of his life, why
should this ancient and trivial moment come back
to visit him? Or bring him back to visit it? Gypsies and psychoanalysts (who are much the same,
although they dress differently) interpret dreams for
us so that we will cross their palms with silver. But
mostly, we can do it for ourselves, as interestingly
as they. What was speaking to him, then? A feeling
he'd had in those flea-hunts of usefulness, of selfless concentration on the poor dog and his troubles.

In that case, the message might not have been about the scene itself but its scale. Was its minuteness the point, the suggestion that all the selfless moments of his life were microscopic? Or it could have been a dream of failure. He wasn't very good at catching the disgusting bugs and most of the time they managed to get away to the forests of the night and jeer at him.

Well, not exactly. But what dreams are exact? Surely there was a sense of the likelihood of failure and a worry about the humiliation of defeat.

No reasonable person would think in such terms. (Are there reasonable people?) Flea powder, flea collars, flea baths…Those work, don't they? (Not very well.) Fleas don't live on a dog but, more cautious, jump on when they are hungry and jump back off as soon as they've drunk enough blood to satisfy themselves. Nasty beasties, but their instincts are smart. Still, they have never figured out a tactic to elude visual inspection and manual extermination. Thus this ritual with the dog stretched out on the floor lying on his back and Vernon kneeling over him. Mostly in the summers. In winters the parasites hibernated or did whatever they do to survive freezes.

But fleas can't be the point. And the meaning of the dream can't be of any use to him, not at this point in life. What interests Vernon is the random vividness of it. A whole life, fairly long, and this is what his sub-consciousness chooses to put on display? It may suppose that the larger and more important events are memorable and that the sleeper does not need reminders of them. The gifts it can offer are instants like these, unimportant but perhaps significant bits of piffle. Or insignificant.

Where do we get the vain idea that anything we do is significant? Say it's a joke then. Fine. Vernon does believe in jokes. They are rooted in his innermost self.

One of Tolstoy's grimmest sentences asserts bluntly that "Ivan Ilych's life had been most simple and most ordinary and therefore most terrible." The more you think about that, the worse it gets. The "therefore" is where the poison is hidden because it relies on the grammar to inform us that the terribilitude is connected to and arises from the first two conditions. Therefore, to contrive any alternative, one must shun ordinariness and simplicity—even if only by these odd memories and lame jokes. They are what he will be letting go of. So long, farewell, *auf wiedersehen*, goodbye.

Or there is a more direct and persuasive explanation. If, as he has long supposed, nothing "means" anything, then why discriminate among memories large and small? Here, he and I arrive at the same place, although by different routes. I have been maintaining that the details don't matter, while he has been presented with a detail, vivid and intimate, and his response is not to welcome it but to dismiss it. What has it to do with him?

An old man, lying in his last bed, perhaps on his last sheets, should have profound questions to ask, never mind answer. He should have some amber drops of wisdom of the kind that certain trees exude, to pass on to his affectionate grandson. But all he gets is a memory of hunting fleas from forty years ago. But that was in another country and besides the dog is dead.

§

No one in the room has had the nerve to bring up the subject of death, even though that is what they have all been thinking about. Or perhaps they think that any mention of his mortality is bad manners. Or even that death itself is in bad taste. Vernon finds this predictable but mildly amusing. He is also relieved because their reticence invites his own and he is not required to tell them that he doesn't much care one way or another, which would annoy them— for his failing (yet again) to meet their expectations. They might even consider it an insult, because if he had any family feeling, any affection for any of them, he'd regret leaving them. Or at least he would have the decency to say so.

How about that for grotesque? And ridiculous. Is the Gnostics' mischievous demiurge joking or not? Yes, is the default answer. His visitors want him to look mournful because that is what they are trying to do, themselves. Trying. They don't feel sad, but if they can fake it, he owes it to them to put forth a reciprocal effort. If it isn't a law of physics it is nonetheless proper behavior. These are painful observations but humorous. What constrains them isn't any lofty deontological rule but mere middle-class convention. (And who called this convention? Alabama casts twenty-fo' votes for Oscar W. Underwood!) How good can the scene be if the actors are not skilled and the script from which they are working is slapdash and unedited?

Vernon is aware that these are ungenerous thoughts. But he doesn't care anymore and should relax a little. Unbidden, however, these observations keep bubbling up from his Pierian spring from which he has drunk but apparently not deeply enough. Should he blame himself? Can anyone control his thoughts, not only censoring any expression of them but even their occurrence? "We have transgressed, we have acted perfidiously, we have robbed, we have slandered, we have acted perversely and wickedly, we have willfully sinned, we have done violence, we have imputed falsely, we have given evil counsel, we have lied, we have scoffed…" One can try not to do any of those things but even as one recites the prayer, he is thinking about doing them.

Has he imputed falsely? Vernon realizes that all his grousing could be distorted, the result of his mood of the moment or of the dour view of things that has been his inveterate habit. (If it weren't inveterate, would it be uninveterate? Non-inveterate? Or just veterate? Sorry.) Maybe he has earned it. In any event it is too late to change and won't last much longer.

If there is anything in this world he might miss, it is this edgy, cranky, critical stream of consciousness, even though it has no apparent point, gets nowhere, and reveals nothing about himself or the world. But it reassures him and reminds him of who he is. People who are non-verbal do this in other ways. With pieces of jewelry they can look at on their wrists or fingers that declare, quietly or stridently, that, yes, it's them. To make it even clearer, some of the pieces are engraved with their names or initials, or a significant date. At moments of stress, you see them rotating the ring on a finger.

What kind of sin is it to scoff? It can be a necessary stratagem for intelligent people trying to hang onto their sanity.

§

Better yet, we can say that these are like the ring of Gyges, but with the opposite effect. Gyges' ring could make him invisible. Rings, nowadays, are for those who feel themselves disappearing, melting into the surround, so they twist the rings on their fingers to restore their visibility and discretely to reassert their existence, if only to themselves.

True? Not true? Either way, it is a pleasing conceit. And Vernon is pleased that he can still be pleased.

§

Is there a plot?

Actually, yes. Vernon's parents bought a plot with room for four graves, but inasmuch as Vernon's intention is to be cremated, his space will not be used. It will pass on along with its intended occupant.

The Vatican has clarified their views on cremation. They still prefer burial of cadavers, so it will be convenient for the heavenly powers to raise them bodily from death when the trumpet shall sound. But cremation has become more popular lately (it is certainly cheaper) and the RCs, looking up from their colas, have come to accept it, but the ashes, or "cremains," are not to be kept on the mantelpiece. Nor should they be scattered to the winds on land or sea. They should be buried in some "sacred place," where they can be venerated. No kidding! Vernon cannot imagine being venerated. It is a primitive and barbarous practice, but that may be part of its charm. You like spooky? They've got an abundance of it swirling through the air like smoke from their censers.

Jews are more straightforward. Cremation? Pfui!

Not allowed under any circumstances. Well, maybe not any. Even the strictest rabbis have said that involuntary cremation is not a sin, so the six million of the Shoah will not have to bear the guilt of it. (See how reasonable rabbis can be!) Also, if you are too stupid to know that cremation is forbidden, you can go right ahead without incurring any blame. Otherwise they are as allergic to cremation as some kids are to peanut butter. Nothing happens to the cremated deadie but the rabbis develop an uncomfortable rash under their beards. Does that clear it up? (Not the rash, the cremation question.) No? So much the better. Now we can have long disputations about the subject. If this, then that. But if that, then the other. Unless that came before this. They can go on like that endlessly, nibbling chickpeas and nodding their heads in earnestness.

Vernon thinks about being in a place of honor in the bookcase in a fancy urn like Keats's maybe. "O Attic shape! fair attitude! with brede/ Of marble men and maidens overwrought…" (Brede? Embroidery or decoration, obsolete not only now but in Keats's time. He was, himself, embroidering.) The bishops, nevertheless, are uncomfortable with urns, which is not surprising inasmuch as the church owns a lot of cemeteries and is in the business of selling plots. Like novelists?

A narrative line, say.

We only find out at the end of our lives whether the narrative amounted to any kind of story. More likely, we conclude that it was a post-modernist jumble, a random collage that is supposed to represent in a coherent way the incoherence of things. Or merely to mimic. (It is a collage from which we never graduate.) We might have had intentions, expectations, or hopes, but how many of us continued in the direction in which we began? The conspectus is one of frustration, compromise, and a relentless diminution of our dreams. We encountered the unexpected and had to adjust. Do that often enough, and the route gets complicated, then obliterated, and at last forgotten.

If there isn't a plot then, as the paranoids maintain, there may be a plot to get us to think so in order for financial advisors, astrologers, and gypsies to earn their livings looking at their charts and crystal balls. The only advantage to believing in predestination is that it relieves us of responsibility. Or guilt, even. Whatever happened, it was fated to happen. There was nothing we could have done about it, was there?

There is an entire academic discipline devoted to the study of narrative. Its practitioners can talk about plots without having to read (or assign) any actual novels. In this cloud-cuckoo-land, there are two quite different traditions: thematic and modal. The former is mainly limited to a semiotic formalization of the sequences of the actions told, while the latter examines the manner of their telling, stressing voice, point of view, transformation of the chronological order, rhythm and frequency.

What? Cut through the jargon and what it says is obvious. There's the story, see, and then there's the manner of its telling. Wow! I adduce all this mostly because it is amusing to consider how the discipline (if not the bondage) caught hold. Narratology is the study of literature by people who don't like reading or are ashamed of themselves for making a living teaching about novels, which are not all that challenging intellectually. (Or are narratologists physicians who specialize in diseases of the nostrils?)

Madness, yes? We can invoke the insanity plea

or the M'Naghten rule. M'Naghten killed Edward Drummond, mistaking him for Robert Peel. (Woops!) The rule holds that people who are not responsible are not responsible. You have to know what you're doing and understand that it is wrong. It is not recognized, however, in Idaho, Kansas, Montana, Utah, and Vermont—perhaps because most of the residents of those states are crazy anyway. Or it could be that their legislators tried hard to enact such an exclusion but couldn't because it was fated for them not to.

§

So. The question arises of predestination. It is interesting (to me) because it poses a practical problem for novelists. Should we work from an outline?

To do so is to imply a universe in which destiny determines what happens.

That is one possibility, of course, but it makes the characters less interesting and reduces all their choices to picturesque irrelevance. Raskolnikov kills Alyona and her sister not because of any inner turmoil but only because Dostoyevsky thought it would be… promising as a donnée. This is what he had scribbled on the napkin and was in his outline. Would it make a better book if, in the tavern, some suitably downtrodden tippler said, "Rodion Romanovich, you are a pitiable character. You are merely a starting place for a novel, as any of us could be for all we know. It is unfortunate, but it's the truth. Relax. Have another drink." Then he has a fit of coughing to demonstrate that he is tubercular, will die soon, and is therefore to be believed.

Ridiculous, you say, but which do you mean? The novel Dostoyevsky wrote (hurriedly, to pay off gambling debts) or the one we have just proposed, less orderly and coherent but for that very reason a more accurate and honest representation of life?

To work from an outline is not merely an artistic decision but a moral and metaphysical one. Fiction is supposed to be a pattern of lies that conveys a higher, more refined truth. But what they may very well convey is only a higher and more refined pattern of lies in which we are invited to participate as unindicted co-conspirators. We take novelists at their word, which does not sound like a sound policy. Say rather that we take refuge in their words because we feel safer there. (But we are not there. If we were, readers of *Moby Dick* would be in danger of drowning. And in *War and Peace* they could burn to death in the fire or freeze in the course of Napoleon's retreat.)

Less extravagantly, we may agree that in the pages of books, we find a more vivid, more reasonable reality than in the one in which we live. But it is too good to be true. A universe in which the good triumph and the wicked fail and in which lovers overcome difficulties to marry at the end is so remote from our experience or that of everyone we know as to be extra-galactic.

Do I get it wrong? Is fiction not a description at all but a prayer of some kind? Are novels the simulacra of an experience we'd prefer? Can we imagine it? Could we stand it? Would we deserve it? Our maculate hearts declare that there is no realistic hope for such a place. In the Vidui, when the penitent asks, "may you grant my share in the Garden of Eden, and grant me the merit to abide in the world to come which is vouchsafed for the righteous," can he imagine for an instant that he could be one of the righteous? Have you ever met one? Do you know anyone who has?

77

Vernon's prospects, however, are quite clear. His outline is the chart that used to hang from the foot of the bed when he was in the hospital and is now on the desk across the room so that nurses and doctors can follow his progress, although it is his diseases that are making progress while he is in retrogression. What is the point of their scrupulous attention? More likely than not, they are acting out of habit. The prison guard who executes the prisoner with a lethal injection wipes the spot first with an alcohol swab to avoid infections. Doctors won't perform this chore, or nurses either, probably. Veterinarians, then? There's nothing in their Hippopotamus Oath to prevent them from killing patients. They do it all the time. (And they have access to the drugs, too, as the prison administrations do not.)

It would be easy enough to make an outline describing Vernon's deterioration. But also impossible, because no outline could plan for the associative play that must be spontaneous and unplanned to be accurate and real. (Yes, Virginia, there is a reel.) He has a tessitura (hardly of the d'Urbervilles), and on that we can build. What has surprised me about him is that his impatience with bullshit, which I like a lot, has turned out to be of great benefit as he confronts the end of his life. Those members of his family who have always resented his bluntness or have been upset by his lack of sentimentality are not worth fretting about. For them, he feels a combination of sadness and contempt but not guilt. They count with him only because they make the good ones like Jacob more impressive. Vernon's impatience with nonsense in life extends, as we might expect, to include death as well so that unless he collapses (or I do) there will be no cheerful peripeteia.

§

There is harpsichord music of Bach, Scarlatti, Rameau, Galuppi, and such like. Reading requires too much effort. Music can recede into the background or be prompted forward according to the moment's requirements. ("Privileged" as academics say.) If his thoughts are interesting, the music is not intrusive. If his brain is quiescent, he can float on its trills and cascading scales. If nothing else, it fends off the silence. The volume is set so that talk is possible, but not necessary and there is no compulsion for visitors to fill pauses with meaningless chatter.

There is also the curious consideration that music is an assertion of time with notes following each other quickly or slowly to an underlying rhythm like that of breathing—the composer's, the performer's, and the listener's. The notes of piano music die, but the composer and the performer can cheat with trills or broken chords that seem to prolong them. Each note is a mini-drama, but all that is going to stop—as every piece of music does. And, no matter how much we may have enjoyed it, we do not go into mourning for it or ourselves. We understood from the beginning that its duration was finite and while we listened we could perceive the passage of time, which was in fact its organizing principle. This is what we learn from an étude. What confuses us these days is that with digitized music one can construct a loop so that it plays on and on for as long as we are in the elevator or in the supermarket aisles. Forever, in fact. This is not acceptable for Bach or even for the Andrews sisters. (Were Patty and Maxine always a little ashamed of LaVerne, whose name betrayed them as trailer trash? Or did that help them, giving a degree of credibility to the "Boogie-Woogie Bugle Boy of Company B?" LaVerne, I think, was the contralto. But in Mound, Minnesota, where they lived, the name might not have been at all remarkable.)

§

"Is it night or day?" he asks. Cole Porter would have maintained that it doesn't make any difference. But it is darker at night than in the daytime. And Vernon remembers having read somewhere that in hospitals there is a spike in the death rate in the wee hours. Hope fades, but then, with the coming of light, revives a little so that the organs keep beating and pumping and doing what they do for another day. Makes sense, but it is evidence that the pathetic fallacy is not always an error of authors. "*Il pleure dans mon coeur/ Comme il pleut sur la ville.*" Verlaine wasn't worried that critics might disapprove of such conceits. His conceit was that they were conceited and should back off. No? *Non?*

"No, no, Nanette" was a musical with Nanette Fabray in it. Vernon never saw it, but the title with its playfully repetitive nasals does stick in one's mind.

In Vernon's anyway. For an instant, he imagines himself muttering aloud, "No, no, Nanette," and being overheard by one of the deathwatch crew. His last words. Good grief! The gossip. The delicious scent of scandal (which is like scandalwood). Who was Nanette, they wonder? The mystery woman with whom he had been in love in his youth but of whom he never spoke? Or with whom he had an affair that lasted forty years? Or whom he married and with whom he had another family someplace far away, like Mound, Minnesota? The evidence is that he bought his sons Tonka trucks, which are made in Mound. But where did he find the time? He was not away from home that often. But then Nanette fades along with Mound. He returns to the question about what time it is.

"Day," says Nurse Rampling.

"Would you open the blinds then?"

She doesn't answer but opens the blinds. Bright sunny day.

Son idée. Is that an *idée fixe*? And is it about set-price menus?

"Is that too bright?" she asks.

"No, it's just right. But get me my sunglasses." The idea of himself in bed wearing sunglasses is engaging. Very Hollywood. (A yachting cap would probably be too much.) He bets with himself that one or another of his visitors will remark about the eyewear within a minute of arriving. (And that's allowing them thirty seconds to notice.) That is what's wrong with them: they have no feeling for the absurd, which may be troublesome but is often attractive and consoling and even sometimes true.

Could Verlaine and Vera Lynn have been distantly related?

§

L'infermière comes to empty his urine bag, change his diaper, and clean him up. She is as professional about it as she can be, but it must affect her. She may have been trained no longer to feel disgust but surely it is unpleasant for her. It is a humiliation they share if only by denying it. A corporeal intimacy, very probably the last one he will experience. It is like those moments of his earliest days, which he cannot remember, when he lay on the changing table to be cleaned and powdered. Do infants understand the great love that must be a part of this transaction? Unlikely, but there is no way of knowing what they know. There may be some residuum that shows itself in a number of adults who confuse the sexual and the excretory. Imagine Sacher-Masoch's toilet training, which must have been excessively harsh or excessively pleasurable. (There is a life-sized statue of him in Lvov. Its face seems to be troubled, as we might expect. Or, knowing who it is, are we biased in that direction as we gaze at its expression?)

These are questions Vernon knows he will not live to answer, but then neither will I. Nothing wrong with unanswered questions, though. They are mysteries, which we have learned to live with and may even need.

§

He sleeps for a while, or it is better than sleeping. He is on that delicious verge between sleep and wakefulness where his mind wanders but he is able to follow its progress. He may not be thinking about anything, but he is thinking. And he is not moving his body. So it is like sleep but with awareness. He may not remember the details, but he knows that he was thinking about shit and the nurse cleaning him up. His attitude was somewhat surprising, but it isn't worth trying to recall. One doesn't want to dwell there. In the little house where everybody goes. (Auden, maybe?) More interesting now is the luxury of languor, which is as close as he ever gets to mindfulness.

These episodes are familiar and Vernon has been enjoying them for years. They were how he dealt with insomnia, lying there very still, letting his consciousness roam off its leash like a dog on a beach in winter that runs this way and that, responding to cues its owner cannot divine. Eventually, the dog tires and returns to sit or lie down at its master's feet, as the mind does, settling down to a doze in which the body participates. Stuff from the newspapers or from his life. Or sometimes both.

§

Ruth is there, another grandchild, a nice enough young woman. Maybe too nice. She has gone to Africa and South America to help the indigent indigenes. Well-intended, surely, but wacko. One of the projects was to teach women prisoners how to make reusable shopping bags out of the flimsy one-time plastic bags from food markets. They sell these so they can buy food, which you'd think the prisons would supply, but they don't. Had Ruthie done this cynically, to embellish her résumé for instance, Vernon would have understood it. As a pure, good work, though, it made him uncomfortable. (Are there not more pressing problems closer to home?) It also made him uncomfortable that she was a vegan. Like Hitler.

But wait a minute. Hold your horses. Hold your water. Water your horses. I seem to have wandered into some semi-real world, where it is dangerous to go. Vulgar empiricism! Even if it is sometimes engaging. I wonder about those women prisoners in Cochabamba (or Quchapampa, if we want to sound primitivo and authentic). If the prison doesn't provide food, then how do the inmates survive? There must be a few with connections to people outside who send money. And then? Trickle-down economics. The ones with

83

the money hire others as servants or bodyguards, and they in turn have their lackeys and dependents. No? I have no idea, but if we knew the facts they would only disappoint us, limiting us and foreclosing speculation.

So ignore the details about Ruth that I have improvised, if not altogether. All that matters is Vernon's amusement at her innocent optimism and her notions about making the world a better place. But as Clemenceau is said to have said (quoting François Guisot, actually), "If [my son] had not become a Communist at 22, I would have disowned him. If he is still a Communist at 30, I will do so then." Guisot is almost forgotten now, except for that Beckett play about waiting for him. So give her time. But time, *messieurs-dames,* is exactly what Vernon doesn't have. This leaves him free to suppose. Coincidentally, he is wearing SuppHose, which they have given him to help prevent blood clots.

For this granddaughter, there is still hope. The jury is out. The doctor is in. The Bronx is up and the Battery's down. The first time he heard that song he didn't get it about the battery being down. But then one day, just walking along somewhere, it hit him. Aha! (There are chemicals in the brain that such flashes of understanding can elicit.) And he has liked that song ever since, more than he would have if there hadn't been the delay in noticing the pun. The paranomasia. The patient has an acute paranomasia and, as with Katisha's left elbow, people come from miles around to see it.

Vernon can allow himself to think she is here voluntarily. Not just because she was ordered to come. (Although she probably was ordered—but she might have come anyway).

"Hi, Grandpa," she says.

" 'lo," he replies.

It is a meme they share that goes way back.

When he goes, it, too, will be gone. Unless of course she decides for one reason or another to keep it and teach it to her children or grandchildren.

§

That smart-assed remark of Clemenceau's (or Guisot's) is a typical French twist. (Those are hairy epigrams.) The French achieved a degree of enlightenment but then, after considerable bloodshed, realized it wasn't such a good thing. Reason is not so important, after all, if it is determined by one's age. Ideas? Mere phases. You think you know something and are ready to die for it (or at least to kill other people) and then you discover that it was merely a stage, the result of your mental astigmatism, a confusion of domains. Or presbyopia, perhaps. (The religion of ophthalmologists?) Or maybe cataracts, which distort colors. Monet painted all those water lilies and then, after his surgery, discovered that they were a different color and much less yellow. But which colors were the *true* ones? The ones he saw before were the ones he painted; how they might read on a spectrometer would not even be relevant.

Will Ruth come to understand this one day? And if she does, will she be terribly disappointed as she recognizes that her efforts of a decade have been a mistake? She thinks she is working for human betterment and then she wakes up to find that she's one of the unknown dwarfs. Along with Dopey and Goofy there are Lefty and Godly. Would Disney allow such a thing?

Why not? Sleepy, Sneezy, and Goofy have conditions of which it is bad form to make fun: narcolepsy, rhinitis, and developmental challenges. Dopey should not be called that derisive name because he is differently abled. Grumpy and Bashful have psychological problems and should not be labeled in this crude way. And Doc? He is not a doctor at all but an example of transference and projection as described by Gabbard, Suler Fenichel *et al.* Indeed, we're not even supposed to call them dwarfs anymore. Little people, I think. "Snow White and the Seven Little People"? Who's left? Happy? (I always think of Mrs. Rockefeller, who wasn't.) He is more probably manic than hedonic.

§

"On Your Toes" is a Rogers and Hart musical. Nobody has written one called "On Your Tush," which would be about me. My PT lady comes to make me exercise every other day. I can't get out of bed, so I'm unlikely to be singing "There's a Small Hotel." What she makes me do is sit on the side of the bed for five minutes, just swinging my legs for four of them and kicking as strenuously as I can for the fifth. This is to keep me from having clots. Which wouldn't be so bad, actually. There are worse ways to die.

The Toes musical was originally supposed to be a movie. With Fred Astaire as Junior, but Astaire turned it down because it was too highbrow and he wouldn't get to wear his white-tie get up.

My therapist's name is Elaine. Elaine Stritch was in the 1954 revival of "On Your Toes." A coincidence? Of course. But I noticed it. But what does it mean? Only that "The truth will set you free" is a nonsense. More often the truth will just confuse you and weigh you down.

§

Why are the grandchildren here at this moment but not the children? Does that require any comment? They have visited and will do so again, but I could have estranged them. Let us take it as a given that the difficulties of growing up make it impossible for any parent to know his child or for any child to know his parent. Can you imagine how surprised Freud must have been—pleasantly and unpleasantly —when he analyzed his daughter Anna?

As Vernon's children passed through various periods of rage and resentment, as all children do, their passions blinded them. Vernon had no clear idea of his own parents until some years after they died, when he could make intelligent guesses about them that were primarily the result of a lifetime of emotional refraction. So with his children, with whom he has learned how to get along and where the conversational bounds are clear if he wants to avoid arguments.

I was tempted to describe these interesting tensions but decided against it. Too depressing. Still it is easier to consider how they might misinterpret an innocent remark and edit himself than to have occasions for arguments or pained silences.

Grandchildren do not carry such baggage and he can talk with them—or some of them—in a spontaneous way. A luxury.

Let us leave his children as stick figures then, like the ones on car windows, mommy, daddy, son, daughter, and dog. (Isn't that sweet?) The two grand-children who have asserted themselves are generalities, with just enough presence, I hope, to be convincing. But if you are not convinced, you are invited to fall back on Vernon's connection with them. And if you don't believe in Vernon? No matter. It's fiction, isn't it? You are sophisticated enough to be comfortable in the land of hypotheses. (Their flag is a faded rectangle of tie-died silk with too many colors to list. Their money is paper notes with portraits of characters from novels, and the word "Velleity" emblazoned on the reverse in script so richly embellished that it is almost impossible to read. Or should it be a simpler "What If?")

V

"The corps and the corps and the corps." That was Douglas MacArthur in his last speech at West Point. Farmer McGregor's version would have been, "The crops and the crops and the crops." Vernon has been playing with this and his own rendering is "The corpse and the corpse and the corpse," although not quite yet. He could also have been involved in a different kind of wordplay, his name, V. Dewey, being an extrapolation from the prayer. *Ashamnu, bogdanu, gozalnu.* We have sinned, we have been perfidious, we have robbed and so on and on. Yes, the words do have meaning but they also have a rhythm, which is at least as important. It is an induction to a trance that feels like meditation. Trance is a focusing of the mind so that everything irrelevant is excluded. It feels as though we have acquired wisdom, although, in truth, what we have done is willfully to put aside most of our knowledge of the world.

We are happy enough to make the trade, because the feeling is so satisfying. A drug addict in pursuit of that very sensation is a contemplative manqué. (A contemplative monkey is on his back.) He wants his fix, but what is he fixing? Himself, of course, but also the world (*tikkun olam*) and he thinks he has attained a perfection in which it is unnecessary to beg for forgiveness.

This, though, is the world we live in. Alas. One way or another we manage to get through our lives. And as Solomon says, "Greater is the day of death than the day of birth." You can check. It's in Ecclesiastes. A puzzling observation that the Chassidic masters explain, saying that the moment of death is the culmination of a life. Newborns are all the same but each dying is different. There may be physical and even mental limitations, but even so this remains the moment of that person's fulfillment. A *telos* with a tallis. Put it another way and think how this is the moment at which a life, stripped down to its core, becomes, as some pious Jews believe, pure soul.

The core and the core and the core.

§

If I were somehow to materialize in Vernon's room and tell him any of this, my guess is that he would dismiss it. But scornfully or sadly? I can't be sure. And he is my guess, after all. All that holds him together is the idea of coherence, in which neither of us believes. He doesn't believe in God, which is what makes his immanent demise interesting. (The devout simply move on to another place, or at least they think so.) He doesn't obey the 613 commandments (Les règles de Jew?) and couldn't even list them. Neither the 365 negative ones nor the 248 positive ones. That 365 coincides with the number of days in the year and the 248, supposedly, with the number of bones and organs in the human body. (In all mammalian bodies? Even pigs?)

Some of these are self-evident; some memorialize historic events; and some, the *chukim*, have no rationale at all but are just arbitrary manifestations of divine will. Some prohibitions are against things no sane person would imagine himself doing. You can't sleep in a cemetery, for instance, for the purpose of being possessed in order to foretell the future. Is there a lot of that? I don't hang out in cemeteries at night, but it might be a good idea to visit some of them once in a while. In darkest Brookline where heretic Jews in their REI sleeping bags, hope to be possessed so as to get the next day's stock prices or racing results. If it is prohibited, there is at least a chance that it works.

Vernon's thought is that if you break one of the commandments, you may as well ignore the rest of them, too. The first is to believe in God. No? You don't? Then you are excused from all of them. From the commandments and from gym, too. Not surprisingly, I find myself largely in agreement with Vernon. I also approve of his epicurean attitude toward death. Instead of asking for forgiveness of sins he has never committed, he is trying to consider his life and what it has amounted to. If anything.

He doesn't believe in predestination, but neither does he believe in free will. Oh, we can choose French fries or a baked potato, but such decisions are not significant enough for us to remember them. The more important choices are seldom based on any cost/benefit analysis, or any rationale at all. Often, he didn't even make them himself. When he was a child and a youth his parents picked out his clothing and his schools. He could express an opinion but that never mattered. They figured that he was a kid and didn't know anything. Even after he graduated and left home, even after they died, they were still telling him what to do and he often obeyed because it was easier than arguing. It is difficult to persuade ghosts to change their minds. It is also sinful. To attempt to converse with the dead is forbidden. (But how about successfully conversing with them? Is that okay? It's like the prohibition against listening to false prophets. How do we know they are false until we have listened to them at least for a little bit? Eh? Oy!)

My favorite sin? I'd have to say the prohibition against bowing down before a smooth stone. That is another thing I'd never have thought of if it weren't forbidden. Not even in Brookline, on the way back from their nights in the necropolis, do the horseplayers and portfolio managers pause to do that. I assume it isn't the bowing down so much as the praying, but what prayers do you offer to a stone? Oh, great stone! You are admirably smooth. You must have been weathering for centuries, for millennia. You must know a hell of a lot! More than me, surely, although that's not a high bar.

I know, it's the idolatry thing that pisses Yahweh off. But this isn't a graven image, is it? It just happens. Like found poetry. Like beautifully gnarled sea wrack from which people make coffee-table bases. Is it okay until you bow down to it? Can you bow down just to examine it? Or to admire it? There is a fine line between admiration and prayer, but there is a line. And if we're talking sea wrack, the line could be in the sand where the metaphor likes to have them.

§

These are not exactly Vernon's thoughts, but... as if. You haven't met him yet, but Aasif is the Albanian practical nurse who comes in at night these days. (Practical nurses are much preferable to the impractical, creative ones.) Vernon has no idea whether Aasif is any good, but he realizes that it doesn't matter much. There is nothing that even Mother Teresa (a fellow Albanian) could do for him. Back in Gramsh, young Ali Aasif was a goatherd and he is a gentle soul, as goatherds tend to be. A caregiver of a kind. The main difference is that in this job he doesn't get to slit the throats of his patients and eat them. But Vernon suspects that he thinks about it. More likely than not, Mother Teresa thought about it, too, and her greatest achievement was keeping such thoughts to herself. Saints alive! [Does that have any meaning anymore? Has it blurred to a mild exclamation? Cheese Louise! Holy Moly! Godfrey Daniels!]

Is this going anywhere? Why has it been dragging its heels? Obviously, the problem is Vernon's. He was and still is about to consider his life. He doesn't want to grade it. (If you fail at life do they make you do it over?) But it deserves thoughtful consideration. The narrative hardly matters. Education, career, and family life take time and attention, but those are only a surface beneath which the actual person lurks, allowing only occasional glimpses that one must be alert to notice and attentive to remember. Often it is an iteration of a piece of behavior that suggests significance, but it could just be the same thing happening twice.

Psychiatrists listen to their patients with what they call a free-floating attention, listening but allowing their minds to wander in the hope of discovering some subtle but meaningful pattern. Vernon's mind is especially talented in wandering. It skitters about looking down (in both senses) at the world of facticity, but from a height at which only a few features of the landscape are recognizable. Is there a place of value in a world of facts? It is too late now for Vernon to reread Wolfgang Kohler's book. Anyway the name is now a joke, Kohler being much better known as a manufacturer of toilets, sinks, and other plumbing supplies. (Go find some value in that, Herr Doctor Professor!) The phenomenological method and the qualitative analysis of experience? Remember to flush.

Vernon is depressed and has been for years. He cannot remember the transition, but there must have been one, sudden or gradual. As a young man he was confident, optimistic, and interested in people, places, and things. His attitudes have deteriorated, however, and he has become cynical and impatient, and although he often resolves not to do it anymore he gets annoyed or angry at incompetent salespeople or waiters. *Ashamnu, bogdanu, gozalnu.*

But it is an oversimplification simply to put him in the category of those who suffer from depression. Yes, it's a disease, but it is also a way of seeing the world. Back in the days of black-and-white photography and actual film, you could use filters to enhance certain effects, to make clouds look more substantial, say, or to bring out contrasts in a seascape. (Does this work with digital photography?) Depression is like one of those filters, distorting in the interest of truth. Depressives speak of the not unreasonable feeling that they are now seeing the world as it is and as they have never before understood it.

Men and women who have gone through a divorce have a similar change in how they perceive the world. A revision, call it. All that they had known and believed crumbled and they realized, in shock but also with some curiosity, the fragility of their lives, the irrelevance of their plans, and their dependence on the whims of fortune. (Or, just as bad, they saw that Fortune was a desperate attempt to rationalize what was fundamentally irrational.) The strangest part of this revelation was the sense that the people who had not (yet) been through a divorce were innocents whose naivety was pitiable. We are all farmers looking up at the sky and hoping for the good weather on which our lives depend.

Had he been offered a "cure" for his depression, he might not have accepted it because such a change would make him more easy-going and more patient with nonsense—in books, on television, and in conversations with people. In other words, it would have made him more tolerant of the second rate, of which there is far too much in the world. He would not have had to clench his teeth every time a newscaster misused the word, "epicenter," which is not the center of the center but a spot directly over (epi) the center of an earthquake.

It would have been possible for him to take credit for his high standards, but he resisted that. They were not an achievement but a burden. He wasn't (quite) a snob but at least an elitist. He demanded more of himself than of others. His upbringing, his toilet training, his education, his psychological wounds… Admit all that and you still have the same personality. And personhood. The defenses we have worked out are not always manifestations of mental morbidity. The thing is that mostly they work. They help us evade and avoid what would otherwise be troubling. They become us; we become them. They are, like a good hat or a well tailored suit, becoming.

So, more important than the narrative line of his life with its vicissitudes and changes in direction and mood, this depression, this fundamental inclination was who he was. It was inconvenient sometimes but it was an assertion of himself. Lying there in the bed perilous, he was pleased that he would never have to change now. Or even try.

§

The nights belong to Aasif. If the days are what is, the nights are conditional, tentative. As if. Not just here in this room but to some extent for everyone, everywhere. There are dreams of course, but there is also darkness into which one can peer and imagine anything. Children see monsters lurking in the corners of their bedrooms or under their beds. Adults see monsters, too, but less literal ones, and more frightening.

Ali presumably is related to Daoud Aziz, who presides over the daylight hours. He is like the eminent empiricist Bishop Berkeley: "What I cannot see/cannot possibly be/ and the rest is exceeding unlikely." His is an odd philosophy. In a French pronunciation, it would come out to *impair*-icist, which is someone who bets the odd numbers at a roulette table. Odd.

Empiricism seems at first to be a minimalist viewpoint, sweeping away all the metaphysical constructions of Platonists. But one can think of it as an assertion of what we can see and touch as a baseline: at least these things are true. For Vernon this is not attractive because what he can see and feel as he lies in bed is not particularly cheerful. Or interesting. Worse, if he is his body, then its truth has little to do with him. He has always thought of it as a container, but now that seems to be an inadequate and misleading metaphor unless we get very elaborate and make it a wine bottle with an imperfect cork so that, sooner or later, air gets into it and the wine turns to vinegar.

He never liked sports and wasn't any good at

them. No great hand-eye coordination and not enough strength for him to do even one chin-up. (Nor did he see any benefit in getting better by practicing or working out.) His dancing was barely passable. Sex was pleasurable, but he couldn't claim those feelings for himself because his pleasures, he assumed, were the same as any man's (any straight man's, anyway) and that sameness made them oddly impersonal, which is a paradoxical aspect of intimacy. *Impair*-sonal. Odd.

He once read an analysis of kissing that proposed the activity as an occasion for the lovers to taste each other, which is why, when the fucking begins the kissing mostly stops. Did he believe this? Or recognize it? He couldn't decide. And he strolled in a leisurely way through the catalogue of the girls and women he had kissed. To do that, it was necessary to list them, and that led him down another path, which was long enough to require that he focus his attention for a while. But that effort was suspended as he found himself wondering what it would be like if he had been one of those basketball players or rock stars who have fucked thousands of eager admirers, sometimes sober but not infrequently drunk or on drugs. If you get to the point where you can't remember most of them, then what was the point?

Those researchers might be on to something, he thought. It seemed that he could remember kisses more vividly than many of the acts of intercourse that sometimes followed. Too powerful to keep? It was like being in a museum and, after several hours, feeling your eyes giving out from a surfeit of lines and colors and...and beauty. That's what the little gardens are for, or the cafeterias, to offer some respite to the patrons whose brains have passed the point of satiety.

The beginnings were different and identifiable. The holding and the stroking and the kissing had, each time, a unique taste and smell, but then as the erotic level rose his attention had narrowed its focus, so that, by the orgasm, he was hardly aware of his partner. Why don't novelists ever say this and demonstrate that they have, at one time or another, paid attention? Some kind of spiders, the black widow maybe, mate and then the female bites off her partner's head. The wonder of it is that the male doesn't care. The praying mantis does this, too. Even if we were to allow that the male spiders and mantises know what is going to happen (do insects *know* anything?) they are undeterred. In the triste post-coital moments when the female is digesting the part of the male she has swallowed, does she have any sense of who he was? Are they self-aware at all? If not, this kamikaze intercourse is less impressive.

Suppose that surgeons have to cut off one or two of your frostbitten toes to stop the progress of gangrene. It is not complicated, then, to assert that you are what remains. You may now lack those toes but that doesn't have much impact on your mind or your personality or your being. When you say, "My toes," to whom does the personal pronoun refer? My hand, my eyes, my head, my heart…The clear implication is that there is a me to whom all these ancillary pieces belong. And yet how far can those diminutions go? If you lose your sight, your hearing, and your ability to speak, does enough remain still to be you? Catholics would vote yes, because they believe in souls, and souls don't need their casings. The body dies and the soul flies free. If you can believe that. This is, perhaps, a question for medical ethicists. Most of them are young men and women who did graduate work in philosophy but could not then find academic jobs, tenure track or not. A philosophy student who specializes in esthetics can become an aesthetician, but their work is mostly in beauty parlors, dressing hair and applying maquillage. Still, customers discuss profound issues with them as if they were metaphysicians.

§

Vernon's body has never been a prize possession and once again it is disappointing him. It has outlasted the bodies of many of his classmates and friends, even younger friends, but that comforts him not at all. He is old, but not quite what doctors call "old old." A strong man will live to fourscore, the psalmist says, but that's not accurate. It's the lucky man who hangs around for a long time in one of those protracted Russian goodbyes. (And the door is ajar and the chill wind is uncomfortable for him, his hosts, and the other guests in the foyer, who wish he would show some consideration and for God's sake leave.)

The body's failures must be worse for those who were athletes or dancers, or who kept fit, running miles a day or pedaling on one of those indoor bicycles. There comes a time for all of them when they realize none of their efforts made any difference. The bodies they lived in and cared for are betraying them as if they had been couch potatoes all those years, eating whatever they wanted and drinking as much as they liked. They realize at last that mortality is not so easily avoidable and that their lives have been, to some extent, a mistake. It is tempting to scorn them, but that would be too easy. It is more interesting to try to understand them and even feel some compassion for them.

Not more virtuous, but just more interesting. He has not been trying to hoard up good deeds to earn a comfy niche in the afterlife. Even as a child, he could not believe that there were ledgers in which supernatural beings totted up columns of figures to make a just judgment about each individual's life and deserts. He tried not to sneer at people who did have faith in such stuff but, again, because it was more interesting to feel some sympathy for these simple souls.

Anyway, the delectable corpus is failing and will, by a slight orthographic adjustment, become a corpse. At least for a little while. Then? Soot. Floating through the air like Casper, the friendly ghost. Which is a way of insisting that there is nothing impressive or awesome about it. Death comes to the archbishop and to everybody else, as well. Anything that happens to everybody cannot possibly be taken seriously. Suppose you die and then meet Casper. How humiliating! Is that the better place? Are children's cartoons the style of the afterlife? If so, to hell with it. Oblivion is better. Properly, that should be Caspar, which comes from the Chaldean word "Gizbar" that means treasurer. Gizbar survives in the Hebrew and still means treasurer. It would be a good name for a dog. "Gizbar, sit! And stay!"

You remember, of course, Guy of Gisbourne. No? The sheriff in Robin Hood—Basil Rathbone in one version, with his voice more nasalized than usual to sound scornful and snobbish.

We are avoiding the issue, circling around it, allowing ourselves only occasional glances. But they are better than nothing. And cumulatively they give us an impression of Vernon's plight, which he, too, recognizes but does not confront directly. The important questions of life cannot be answered by squibs from

Chinese fortune cookies. (A great fortune cookie, that.) Better than "Don't forget to floss," or "Eat more kale," which I expect to find one day, nestled in the whorls of the cookie. But Vernon knows. He knows. And these fitful feints, his attempts to put flightiness aside and at last come to terms with his life, if not his death, are the best he can manage.

The ancient Greeks never had to floss. They didn't live long enough to have to worry about periodontal disease, which is maybe the upside of a down. Nowhere in Homer is there any reference to Greeks or Trojans pulling a thread through the spaces between their teeth. Gum problems are part of the price we pay for longevity. And arthritis and cancer. Bad hips and bad knees. Diabetes. Obstructive lung disease. Arrhythmia. Enlarged prostates. Isn't it extraordinary that with all these hints (or, actually, billboards), most people maintain their state of denial and refuse even to consider the inevitability of death?

For them, too, pity or scorn. As with the witch and the happy boy and girl on barometers, which one comes out of the little door depends on the weather. Will the weather be good or bad, which? Which is the time of the witch? Let me taste your ware? My what? Your ware. Where? What? Which?

§

The tree of knowledge in Eden, remember that? The knowledge might not have been of good and evil but simply of life and death. Perhaps the two trees were conflated. Or, to be fanciful, their branches reached out to intertwine so that together they made a single canopy overhead, which is the source of the confusion. Animals, after all, do not know they are going to die. They don't think about death because they don't think and have a limited notion of futurity. But our knowledge of mortality is not what God intended. This was Satan's work, after all. And Eve's. It was not a gift, then, but plunder. And we cannot tell whether or not the burden of our having it makes us any better off. Call it an oleo of marginal benefit, useful only to those wise enough to accept it and include it in their views of life. For the rest? It is unimaginable, so they do not try. They pretend to themselves and each other that it is not going to happen to them—even though the dumbest of them knows he is kidding himself. Better to know. And better yet to know and to assent, for this is the beginning of wisdom—and also the end. Anyone who has truly acknowledged his condition in the universe and the brevity and insignificance of his life has reached what may be the highest possible level of understanding. This, surely, is a very lofty standard, but there is the Vidui, which does not require sophistication to recite, and which declares that assent, whether the dying person saying the prayer means it, feels it, and understands it or not.

It is one of the strange facets of Judaism that it doesn't matter what you believe, just as long as you behave in certain ways, eat certain things and refrain from eating other things, wear certain articles of prayer like the *tallit*, the phylacteries, the *kippah*. Observe those 613 commandments and you are home free. In like Flynn, except that Flynn is probably Irish. Even if you suspect that the entire regimen is a foolishness, your ticket is punched. God may actually prefer the correct behavior of a non-believer who does these things simply because this is what Jews do. Every observance is an *acte gratuit*, a performance of a duty. If I were God, I'd approve of such a drama in which the person overcomes his intellectual objections forty or fifty times a day to offer instead an irrational, blind obedience.

But what kind of sacrilege is it to begin a sentence with "If I were God?" Enormous. Unforgivable (if there is such a category). This offensive idea, however, is the basis of all theology, isn't it? The people to whom God speaks directly wear tinfoil hats, preach at entrances to the subway, and are more fervent than the saner ones in skullcaps and *tallitot* (or, in Yiddish, *talleisim*) who merely suppose that in the distant past God may have spoken to Moses.

But did Moses have a sense of humor? Did he never suspect, even for a moment, that God might be putting him on? And us? We are all agreed that God is given to outrageous jokes—as with his command to Abraham about killing Isaac. And then, at the last minute, there's the ram in the briar patch (Br'er Rabbit's?) and God doesn't even have to say "April fool!" or whatever the heavenly equivalent might have been. (This is not the usual reading of the story, but it makes sense and is what Sarah must have thought. And, later on, Isaac, if they ever told him about it.) [*Sha! Die kinder!*]

§

These details are the grit some birds have in their stomachs to help digest their birdseed and it doesn't much matter what the grains of sand or small pebbles are made of. Similarly, in novels, the characters, the dialogue, the settings, and even the actions are irrelevant. What the author has to communicate floats above all that grist and, ideally, should not even be written down.

Think of Dutch Renaissance paintings, which communicate an ordered tranquility for which there can be no figurative representation. Even to talk about tranquility while you stand in front of the canvas is too intellectual and diminishes the picture. So, *sha*! Just stand there and stare at what is in front of you. To be smart you must acquire stupidity.

More grit. Aasif comes in to take his vital signs. But Vernon objects. "What's the point? When I'm dead there won't be any blood pressure and the temperature will fall quickly enough for you to be able to tell without any instruments. And there isn't any information you need for a treatment plan because there isn't any plan."

"That's all true, but I have to do my job," Aasif says.

"Why?"

"For the money."

"Ahh! An honest man. Then do me a favor and just write down some plausible numbers. You can repeat whatever the last numbers were. No one will know. They may not get credit for it but dead men are good at keeping secrets."

Aasif thinks about it for a few seconds. What the hell! If he's going to sign the chart "Aasif" it might as well be as if, no?

VI

There was a poet many years ago who published one book, quite good, and then disappeared from sight. Murray Noss, his name was. I heard a rumor that he drove around the south, staying at old traveling salesmen's hotels and sitting on their verandahs where he would write poems on a MAGIC SLATE (trademark by Slate Computing, LLC) and then whoosh them away. True? True that I heard the rumor. But true that he actually did this? There was a Murray Noss, but the rest? I am an unreliable narrator (I swear: trust me) and I am referring to what is a good but unverified story. Therefore the image shimmers in the indeterminacy in which literature thrives. The specificity of the trademark information is supposed to lull you into accepting the rest of the tale, but that's an old trick and you should not be taken in by it. I do hope, however that you may be interested in the mechanics. The magic is not in the moment when the poor bastard on stage pulls the bunny out of the hat but in the long weeks of training the bunny to hold still in the hat long enough for him to do his spiel. Is it harsh training? Or does the rabbit get treats when he does what he does (i.e. nothing at all) properly? It can't be hard to intimidate a rabbit, but then they are not all that bright, so it may take many tedious hours (both for the trainer and the rabbit) to get the animal to understand that he is not supposed to move. Do they, when they are not working (training or performing) have an otherwise friendly relationship, owner and pet?

The whoosh is more important than the poem, as the elegant Mr. Noss understood. If it were a Swoosh, that would be altogether different. Swoosh is a trademark of Nike and is worth more than $26 billion. You can buy an awful lot of poetry for that. Or a lot of awful poetry.

So take all these details and ignore them. Or think of them as dummikvots, which is what one of my professors used to call "dummy quotes." While he was writing, he didn't bother to look stuff up. He'd just think for a moment and decide what Kant would have said. Or ought to have said. Then, when the essay was finished, he'd give it to a graduate student to go to the library and find somewhere in the works of Kant or perhaps the letters something close to what he had put in the essay. Almost always, the grad student could find it, often word for word. Very rarely, it was a line from some other philosopher that had slipped in. But the professor's batting average was amazingly good.

Consult your own lives then and find suitable replacements for the dummikvots I have set down. Your own experiences will speak to you better than anything Vernon and I could make up. And you will care about them more because they are yours.

No, no, I'm not accusing you of indifference to the plight of your fellow man. This is what everybody does, thinking about himself, then maybe his family, and so on, less and less as the circle gets wider. Greater love hath no man than to lay down his life for a friend, John says, quoting Jesus. Another God-joke, I fear. Those disinclined to sacrifice themselves may not show greater love, maybe, but greater intelligence. That's the line we are supposed to supply. The point of the gag. Jesus wasn't just horsing around; he wanted to see if anybody was paying attention. Or which ones weren't. You have to separate the wheat from the goats—which is not difficult.

§

After the whoosh, I expect Noss felt good. He'd written the poem, which is satisfying, at least for a few minutes. But the poem was gone, so that now he couldn't read it over with an adversarial eye and try to find places that could be improved. That part is less fun. And he didn't have to worry about rejections from stupid editors, or unflattering reviews, or the lack of any reviews whatever or readers for that matter, all of which are not fun at all. All the pleasure, then, and none of the mess. A good deal, I suggest. But was there no value in the poem? Get real. Whole book of poems, many of them, are available for $.01 at Amazon. A penny for their thoughts! There's a $3.99 shipping charge, so they are really four dollars. But what does "really" signify? L. L. Bean offers Free Shipping, but that only means that the cost of shipping is factored into the selling price. Not free, then, unless you are not using the old bean—which is what old Bean is counting on.

At any rate, if thirty or forty poems are worth one cent, then a single poem, short, a page long (that's the limit of the MAGIC SLATE) is worth a tiny fraction of a penny. To hell with that, Noss may have thought, and with particular pleasure done the whoosh thing. No academic misreadings or befuddled student essays. It's a picnic without the ants, and if you're shrewd you learn to accept that. Enjoy it, even. I don't believe there are any ants in *"Le Déjeuner sur l'herbe"* are there? Not even those tiny red ones, for verisimilitude. Or as a joke. Manet is already making a joke, with the two dandies dressed to the nines while the women are *nue*. (Nu?) And yes, there is a second woman, in the stream in the background. One could call the piece *"Absence de fourmis."* ["Then word goes forth in Formic:/ 'Death's come to Jerry McCormic.' "]

There is such a thing as "found poetry," when a poet finds something somewhere, on a billboard maybe, and discovers that it is, as is, a poem.

Noss was a pioneer of the opposite genre, "lost poetry."

And he, too, is lost. Dead, probably, the whoosh of the CELLOPHANE having taken him to wherever his words went. A good way to go, Vernon thinks.

Quick, painless, un-messy. And prettier than having one's flesh thaw, melt, and resolve itself into some disgusting deliquescence.

Vernon's own demise will almost certainly be uneventful. If there is pain, there are medicines for that, and "terminal sedation" is always a possibility. It is almost as good as death, except for the pesky continuations of respiration and circulation. (And, of course, increases in the bill.) It is not illegal. It is less "dying" than "passing away," which is not so blunt.

Mimsy, maybe, like the modest coverings of the "legs" of pianos in Victorian days. But there is no point in niggling about euphemisms anymore.

They are no longer Vernon's problem. Neither is global warming nor the influx of refugees in Europe. He is excused from all that and any of the other modish issues journalists chew over to no purpose and no end. He has never paid much attention but now he doesn't have to feel even minor twinges of guilt.

If there is nothing he can do, he has nothing to worry about. Epicurus, again. His past life would have a better claim to his attention if only he could contrive some orderly, systematic way of recovering it. But his memories are fragmentary and unrelated and their quality is not reliable. His moods dictate which of them will appear to him, the ones that make him proud or ashamed. Beyond the particular dreams, though, he has a general regret that he did not live more intensely and wasn't more aware. You have one life to live, as the soap opera kept saying, and the least you can do is to pay attention. (OLTL the cast called it. And it's dead now.)

§

Okay, okay. So you're dying, and the chances are that at least sometimes you are bummed out by the idea, however unclear it may be. Your mood influences—or produces—those moments that are still the occasion for chagrin. And they are even further depressing. In such hopelessness and despair, there is some comfort sometimes for some people:

> For the sin which we have committed before
> You by frivolity.
> And for the sin which we have committed
> before You by obduracy.
> For the sin which we have committed before
> You by running to do evil.
> And for the sin which we have committed
> before You by tale bearing.

109

For the sin which we have committed before You by swearing in vain.

And for the sin which we have committed before You by causeless hatred.

For the sin which we have committed before You by embezzlement.

And for the sin which we have committed before You by a confused heart.

For all these, pardon us, forgive us, atone for us.

Tough stuff, especially that last one. To have a confused heart is a sin? Putting it another way, to be yourself is a sin, to admit honestly to your thoughts and feelings is a sin, to be alive is a sin.

For that sin, however, there will soon be remission.

Does that help?

§

His mind wanders around the apartment to visit rooms he has not seen for some time and probably never will again. He thinks of his closet with the shirts and suits he doesn't need anymore. And the ties. All those pretty and expensive ties (not always the same ones). He could ask Aasif to go and fetch him one. Let him pick one at random. (Surely their tastes in neckwear will not be identical.) He imagines the reaction when visitors see him in bed in sunglasses and a tie. They will confer. They will discuss whether he needs a psychiatric evaluation. Maybe. But any course of therapy would take more time to be effective than he has left to give it. If that is true, then any evaluation would be pointless. Crazy, even. But would his family be tough-minded enough to realize this?

Aasif brings him a tie, bright yellow with small red flowers on it. A tie he hasn't worn for years. Brooks Brothers, intended for spring or early summer. But Vernon decides that this may have been as good a choice as he could have made, because it is striking and they can't help noticing it. Around his neck, above his johnnie, it may even scare them. Good. And they will try not to show their concern but will fail. Very good. It is possible that the term johnnie came from the fact that if a patient is wearing one of these open-at-the-back hospital gowns, it is easier to help him go to the bathroom (the john), but there is some doubt about that, because it is too easy—if that makes any sense.

§

I put it to you, ladies and gentlemen of the jury, that what we have seen demonstrates a plot. With malice prepense. And that my entire testimony has been a tissue of lies ("tissue" is to be pronounced so that it rhymes with "miss you" and is snottier and menacing, like Basil Rathbone). There is no question but that what we have before us is a proposal for an action that may or may not succeed. Vern will learn, as will we. But even at so elementary a level, it is plottish. (If there was a Popish plot, it surely follows that there might have been a plottish Pope. How is it that in the long history of religious disputation, no one has remarked on this before?) It is your duty to convict, for then the defendant will have a conviction, which is more than most of us can claim. If the glove fits, wear it. I rest my case.

And myself.

III

But I am not done. It is time for me to come out to address you honestly, even if it means violating all the rules of fiction. It is prohibited in courtrooms for a lawyer to vouch for his client. He must prove the defendant's innocence with evidence or by impeaching the prosecutor's evidence, but he cannot say, "Take my word for it," or "I swear that this is the truth." To do so would be to inculpate himself, so that if his client is adjudged guilty and sent to jail, the advocate would have to go with him.

Nonetheless, even if it is a violation of protocol and genre, I come out from behind the scrim to speak to you from downstage with the lights open white. But before I do that, let us consider the term "scrim," which means either a finely woven lightweight fabric, often semi-transparent but sometimes painted, or else a heavy, course material used for reinforcement in both building and canvasmaking. In its first meaning, it comes apparently from the Walloon. The origin of the second meaning, except possibly as an opposite of the first, is unknown. But that bolus of information, although true, is not what I came out to tell you.

I am about to impart a more pertinent truth, but it is interesting to observe that a truth in a context of fiction is pretending to *be* fiction, and that pretense itself makes it fictional or, bluntly, untrue. So I can't win, which may suggest that you can't lose, as Three-card Monte players try to fool you into thinking. Their shifts change, you see, and when Aziz goes off duty, Aasif comes on, and I can only tell them apart if I know what time it is.

Anyway, what I'm telling you is that there was an event in the actual world that prompted this farrago. (Long away and far ago?) I went to a memorial service for a friend and listened to his children and grandchildren say affectionate and admiring things about him, which may or may not have been true. It is true, though, that they did say these things, sometimes winging it but sometimes speaking with notes or from a complete typescript. You don't need to know what a good guy he was, but take it from me (vouching again) that I liked him well enough to put on a suit and schlep over to the memorial chapel to sit through this, even though I knew that it couldn't do him any good anymore or me either. I knew this but still went because it would have been disrespectful not to him but to my memory of him not to go. In other words, it was utterly pointless, but I was rewarded for my irrationality and got something out of it after all. The guy's widow, speaking to her brother who had flown in from somewhere (Mound, Minnesota, for all I know), told him a detail that I happened to overhear. Odd and unexpected, it was striking enough to bestir my thoughts to produce a vague idea for this book. Or an idea for this vague book. Actually a vague idea for this vague book, which sounds redundant but isn't. Vagueness comes in many forms, as the *nouvelle vague cineastes* insisted. Clarity can only betray it.

I am old enough to know what to do with such promptings, which is to tell them to get lost. More accurately, I try to lose them, not think of them and forget them. Most of the time, I can do this without much trouble. But some, the pesky ones (the ones with a pess key) keep coming back to pull at my sleeve, impish, sly, rude, and obstinate. (The ideas, that is, not the sleeve.)

There is an old vaudeville routine in which the straight man tells the funny man that he can learn

French in ten minutes. They argue for a while and to demonstrate the straight man begins the lesson. He teaches his partner to say *"gai,"* an actual French word that means "cheerful." Then the second word in his lesson is *"avec,"* also a real French word, a preposition meaning "with." Then for the kicker, he has the funny man put the two together, *"gai avec,"* and the joke is that he is no longer speaking French but Yiddish and is saying "go away." Fairly sophisticated for burlesque houses, but the comedians liked it well enough to keep it in the routine. So do I. *"Gai avec,"* I say, to these ridiculous ideas that have occurred to me. (What other kind would occur to me?)

Now and then one of them persists, showing up at unpredictable times and places, less bothersome but still there, like Hitchcock getting off a bus. I am used to it. And despite my better judgment (do I have one?) I find myself wondering if this may not be connected to something. Even something "important." (The quotes are apologetic: I never think that anything I think would be important.) I can't imagine what could be triggering this idea. If I could figure that out, I'd be able to banish it from my mind. But it has some secret agent in there encouraging it and helping it.

I argue: I'm too old for this; I'm tired; this whole business is pointless. But finally I see that the only way to get rid of the idea will be to sit down and do something about it. (Maybe it will be something short. Or something so awkward that after making an honest effort I can quit.)

You believe any of that? Neither do I.

§

His wife? Ex-wife? Should we supply him with one of these? My first (and second) inclination was to keep mum about these matters (and about his mum, too), lest anyone confuse or conflate him and me. (Confusion would be unintentional; conflation, malicious.) But that wouldn't have been satisfactory. There would have been a lacuna. (La Cuna would be a good name for a nightclub catering to scholars.) So my third thought was to include a former wife at least in a minimal way. We don't need any details about her: she is only of relative (ho ho) importance. The interesting thing is Vernon's speculation about her motives. Has she shown up out of sympathy? (Unlikely.) Or to provide what comfort she can to their children? (Possibly.) Or, is she using that as an excuse for her presence and the opportunity to gloat? (Probably.) An ex-wife doesn't have to say any words. They float over her head like a cartoon balloon: "I'm still alive and you're dying! We'll put you in a grave and after everyone else is gone I'll come back to dance on it. A tarantella with a lot of stomping."

Is she really that vindictive? Not always and not with everyone. But divorced couples generally dislike each other. Antipathy comes with the decree. The trouble is that they know too much about each other and with that abundance of information can plausibly interpret even innocent words or gestures and impute to them the worst possible motives. Beside that, they know all of each other's buttons and can push them whenever they like, setting off a wave of rage or depression in their former spouse. Or by accident or just out of habit.

The only thing that allows us to behave in a civil

way with other people is our ignorance, Vernon supposes. If we knew their minds and souls as well as divorced couples know each other's, we would all be driven to continual, indiscriminate violence. All ages are dark and all lands are badlands, if only we admit the hidden truths of our lives together. We learn defenses and acquire skills in inflicting pain and we manage to get along (barely) from day to day in a condition that isn't peace but, at best, a truce that is often violated.

There is a prohibition in the Talmud somewhere against a divorced man being in the same room (or maybe even house) with his former wife. To avoid temptation of once more responding to old familiar cues and having sex? I used to think that was the reason but as I got older I realized that it was to prevent an iteration of hostilities between people who were armed with too much knowledge of each other's habits and foibles, weapons that cannot be checked at the door. In any event, she is not in the room but has flown up and is staying in their son's spare room. Thus, even without a visit she has contrived a visitation and triggered these unhappy ruminations about life.

He wants the children around him, but her presence and his impending death nudge them away from him and closer to her. When he is gone, it will only be her existence that keeps them from being orphans and next in line for the attention of the angel of death. None of them believes in the angel or attributes to death the intelligence the trope assumes. But there is a new feeling of nakedness and vulnerability. It may not be rational but is nonetheless real, Hegel's famous wisecrack notwithstanding.

At a slightly more abstract level, Vernon is intrigued by the realization that even if she is not here in the room, she is here in the room—more so than some of the people, who are physically present, clustered around the bed. She stains the time past and blights the time to come.

§

As biography (auto- or allo-), none of these details is particularly compelling, but do not forgo the foregoing. "Do not be misled by the fiendish simplicity of my remarks," as Husserl may have said. Or was it Merleau-Ponty?

We are dealing with a paradox of a certain charm, no? Take it as the best I can do, in exchange for which I shall continue to think of you all with gratitude and esteem. It remains the case that either he or I had the idea about wearing the tie and then, as can sometimes happen, were prompted to enlarge and improve upon it. Second thoughts have the advantage of standing on the shoulders of their predecessors so that they have a marginally better view of the parade. It was only in the fifth draft of *The Idiot* that Dostoevsky figured out that Myshkin was a prince. [Imagine the labor of just copying out *The Idiot* five times in longhand.] And it was only after having a second thought with tea and his favorite crackers, that Alexander Graham Bell realized, "Ah, I see! You have to have two of them!" There is an online course: *Améliorer son idée*, mostly about feedback, but the implication is that the main purpose of an idea is to discover what its progeny may be or how this one will have improved when it returns. We'll meet again, some *son idée*.

Having been graced with this splendid enhancement of his original notion, Vernon directs Aziz to

117

put the tie in a drawer for now. Later he will undertake his performance and will not care in the slightest what his family says or thinks or how or whether they will react. This is a healthy sign for it means that he will be expressing a self that has been dwindling perhaps but still exists and operates in the present continuous tense. "I am going," rather than simply "I go." It has a hint of the dramatic even though both will eventually find completion in "I am gone."

§

Vernon's relations with his relations are complicated. (Nabokov corrects Tolstoy to point out in *Ada* that all unhappy families are alike, too.) Vernon's trouble is that he expects a great deal of them because they are his family, his blood, and they generally fail to meet these expectations, so he is often annoyed with them. Repetition has formed a neural channel through which his perceptions flow, just as the passage of water over time carves into the earth to form brooks and sometimes canyons. Here again, the family is failing him and seems to have no realistic idea what death could be. Vernon doesn't believe that one must be terminally sick to confront death. It lurks everywhere, all the time. *Mors ubique est.* Also, *timor mortis conturbat me.* But the only way to fight such conturbation is to face it unflinchingly. We all die, but the manner of our deaths is various. Family members used to insist that doctors lie to their patients so as not to extinguish hope. This assumes that the patient is stupid enough to collude in this deception. He knows, he has always known. We all have known. What hope can mortals have of immortality?

Most of the time, it isn't the loss of hope that is

decisive but more simply fatigue. At a certain point it makes no sense anymore to take in food and water and turn them into shit and piss. To endure the probing and the piercing. To swallow the endless capfuls of pills and capsules of different colors and shapes. Why in heaven's name? Why on earth? Vernon understands, as the doctors and relatives do not, that it is all otiose. Wednesday, Thursday—what difference does it make? Or maybe Tuesday / is my bad-news day. You can reach a point, where Death becomes your friend, offering his hand and his kind kind of surcease.

For the moment, however, Vernon has an answer to the persistent question about the purpose of life. Even if that purpose seems trivial, if it has importance for Vernon, that is sufficient. He can contemplate a moment in the future in which he can accomplish something, effectuate a plan, and see how it turns out. Or, in the bluntest terms, live. The way you pick your nose, /the way you shit and pee/ the way you soil your clothes.../No, no, they can't take that away from me!

You don't believe me? Look at it this way. I've told you that we're talking about a small thing, a kind of joke, but you are interested, if not fascinated, and curious about what is going to happen. How will it turn out? What will it mean (if anything)? You are once again caught in the nets of narrative, which means that Vernon's vitality is still full of élan. Or is it the other way around?

We could continue to pass the time (what choice is there? to let the time pass us?) with this persiflage, but in answer to Vernon's prayers I shall spare us further delay and come right out with it. And let us say Amen. He instructs Aziz to fetch his light blue silk shirt and his gray flannel suit from the closet, and also his shoes and socks. And that tie in the drawer? Bring that, too. Then he asks his help in getting dressed.

"I can't do that, sir."

"Why not?"

"It's not in the orders."

"Then it isn't forbidden, is it?" Vernon asks.

Aziz grudgingly admits that is so.

"Then help me."

It is a complicated business, with all those lines and tubes that have to be taped into place or temporarily pulled.

"But how long can you continue this way?" Aziz asks.

"It doesn't have to be long. Ten minutes or so. Get me my wrist watch, would you?"

He sets his watch and winds it. Now he is lying down on top of the coverlet, not at all uncomfortably, as he waits for the doorbell to ring.

"Before you let them in, help me stand up."

This takes some effort on both their parts to manage but, as Aziz goes to open the door, Vernon is standing beside the bed, upright, a person again, at least for the moment.

They come in and his son asks, "What are you doing?"

"Nothing," he replies. "Just standing here."

"But you're dressed."

"So are you."

"What's the point?"

"I could ask you the same thing," he says and he begins to laugh, a gentle chortle that too soon turns into a gurgled cough. "All right," he says to Aziz, "help me out of this."

He half-sits, half-collapses onto the edge of the bed where Aziz can help him undress.

"What did you mean by that, Grandpa?" Jacob asks.

"Mean? What do you mean, mean? What does it mean to get dressed in the morning?"

"That's different."

"Is it?" Perhaps a little too sharply.

Jacob has the good sense to back off. And the others, who have been puzzled or disapproving, are reluctant to press him further. Good.

And what are their names? What difference does it make? Do we know the names of the assassins in Richard III? Do we feel deprived? But all right, you want names? Harry, Larry Barry, Manny, Moe, and Jacob-not-Jake-or-Jack. And besides Ruth there are Violet, Rose, Daisy, Amaryllis, Heather, and Holly. Is that better? They are the ones reporters refer to as "the loved ones," although that is making unwarranted assumptions. Or editorializing. Call them *staffage* and although they serve our purposes, they are shy. To individuate them would be to intrude. (Besides, have you ever heard of a Jewish Amaryllis? Amaryllis Felzenfeld?)

For that matter, do we even know what actual disease Vernon suffers from? Does it make a difference? The fight to cure cancer, if we were to win it, would only change the notations on death certificates, but there would still be death certificates. The fight against death is what they want, but if we put it that plainly, its absurdity becomes clear. Without cancer, we'd die of heart disease, or stroke, or obstructive pulmonary disease. Or something more exotic, maybe, some ailment of interest to the physicians. The patients don't much care and certainly do not take pride in the rarity of their affliction. They don't even get credit for it. Even supposing that it is some medical novelty, the doctor's name will be attached to it, not that of the patient—unless he is Lou Gehrig or St. Vitus. The sufferer looks up in bafflement as Dr. Ackerman (for instance) tells him, energetically but managing not to grin, "You have my tumor!" The man on the examination table is not enlightened. The good physician explains it in simpler words, telling him that in his larynx he has a kind of verrucous carcinoma that afflicts those who chew tobacco or, in Taiwan, betel nuts. It is exophytic, broadly implanted, and fungating in aspect, with papillary fronds. There, the patient is better informed but he doesn't know any more. He still believes he is being punished by God for having chewed tobacco during much of his life.

There are endless variations of this poignant doctor/patient transaction, and for Ackerman you can substitute others. Abderhalden–Kaufmann–Lignac syndrome (aka Abderhalden–Lignac–Kaufmann disease) is one, and we can imagine the angry letters that Lignac and Kaufmann sent to each other and then to Aberhalden, who couldn't decide. I also like the implied drama in Adams–Stokes syndrome (aka Gerbec–Morgagni–Adams –Stokes syndrome, aka Gerbezius–Morgagni–Adams–Stokes syndrome, aka Stokes–Adams syndrome). Not collegial, maybe, but funny, which is more to the point.

I don't believe that there are marches for (against) any of these complaints. Or telethons or lapel ribbons.

After all that effort of getting dressed and, albeit briefly, out of bed (for many of us the most difficult task of the day), Vernon finds himself speculating about whether or not any of them got it? For the ones he likes, he has hopes. And the others? Fuck 'em. If you gots to ask, you never gets to know. Fatha Hines? Duke Ellington? Louis Armstrong? Maybe they all said it at one time or another. But probably not at the same time

Vernon is not dense and he knows that he has been avoiding thinking about his death. Or, actually, his life. (Same thing, no?) What has it amounted to beyond this mildly amusing stream of semi-conscious wordplay? Everyone (nearly) has parents, children, wives and lovers, and victories and defeats, and therefore these accidentals do not distinguish them. The old sepia photographs, no longer on a wall but now in a box in the bottom of a closet, show these family groups, but it is impossible to read the expressions on any of the faces. And the expressions are who they are. If in the end that is all there is, is it enough? (Enough for whom or for what?) Vernon is not dissatisfied, which is no mean accomplishment. Because of the pitter-pat of patterned patter, his existence has been slightly richer than those of most men and women. He knows this and is grateful. Or rather say content. He is. And as we all know, "contents may settle in handling."

Do not turn away from our supplication, for we are not so impudent and obdurate as to declare before You, Lord our God and God of our fathers, that we are righteous and have not sinned. Indeed, we and our fathers have sinned.

Yeh-yeh. Yeah. Yes. Amichai adds to the confession: " 'We have forgotten, we have remembered' —two sins / that cannot be atoned for. They ought to cancel each other out / but instead they reinforce each other."

§

He turns his head. He turns away from his supplication. If his bed were next to a wall, he'd be looking at the wall. He'd have preferred it that way but it is not worth complaining about. He closes his eyes. Or one might more precisely say that his eyes close, because he is no longer issuing the orders.

It isn't the same day as his demonstration to himself as much as the world that he could dress and get out of bed, but the evening of the next day. The hours that elapsed were not particularly trying. He wasn't in pain or even discomfort. But they were tedious. He was bored. He had had enough. He thought of men and women who lay languishing on the last day of December hoping to survive long enough to qualify for another year's tax benefits for their estates. An absurd reason for hanging on but at least a reason. You may not tell your doctors everything, or even your psychiatrist, but surely you should be forthcoming with your accountant. CPAs don't do CPR, but they don't have to, do they? Do they ride the Canadian Pacific Railway? Do they do Cell Phone Repair? Listen to Colorado Public Radio? Or follow Civil Procedure Rules?

It is not a promising vein to mine. Mind but vain. To have been and not to have been in Wein would have been to have gone in vain. He gives up.

His breathing stops. After a few seconds it resumes with a large inhalation and a corresponding exhalation. More seconds pass—nine? ten? Then one more breath.

Then he dies.

Born in White Plains, NY, ***David R. Slavitt*** was educated at Andover, Yale, Columbia, and *Newsweek*. When he was 30, he "lit out for the territory" (Cape Cod) and commenced as a freelance writer. He has published 120 books: poetry, novels, criticism, and translations (from Hebrew, Greek, Latin, French, Italian, Spanish, Yiddish, and Portuguese). He lives in Cambridge, MA, with his wife and a cat.